SUMMER PRINCESS

DARK FAE #1

SLOANE MURPHY

Sophie.

Embrace your inner

Royal.

Summer Princess
Dark Fae #1
Copyright © 2020 Sloane Murphy

Published by Hudson Indie Ink
www.hudsonindieink.com

Summer Princess/Sloane Murphy - 2nd ed
ISBN-13 - 978-1-913769-07-9

To those who have learned to forgive the ones that have wronged you.
To those who have been betrayed and learnt to love again.
This is for you.

GUIDE TO THE ISLES OF RIVINEA, HOME OF THE FAE

Ringa–north of the Isle Eressea - Winter Court:

Ruled by King & Queen Vasara

Prince Cade Vasara–heir to the throne and Commander of the Winter Armies

Prince Rohan Vasara

Avaenora–south of the Isle Eressea - Summer Court:

Ruled by King & Queen Daarke

Prince Erion Daarke - heir to the throne and Lieutenant of the Winter Armies

Prince Edimere Daarke (twin)

Princess Emelia Daarke (twin)

Sintera–small isle to the west of Eressea—Autumn Court

Ruled by King Levoya & Queen Nayla Verano

Princess Araya Verano

Talia Natsu and Arabella Verano – cousins to Araya and taken in by the Royals after their parents were killed in the war

Timerrya – small isle to east of Eressea – Spring Court
    Ruled by King Tristain & Queen Varah Samhradh
    Centra Samhradh
    Yasmina Samhradh

Hunters – half Demon, half Fae creatures, bound to serve and protect the Fae
    Elves – sworn enemies of the Fae, live to the east of the Isles of Rivinea, in the lands of Shani

PROLOGUE

Emilia

Age 9

"*E*mmyyyyyy. Come out and play! Cade and Rohan are waiting. I don't want to kick their butts if they're mean to you because we're late," Edi whines from my doorway. I finish pulling my hair into a ponytail and sigh.

"It's not my fault Mother makes me wear stupid dresses all the time. I had to get changed. Come on, let's go now, before she sees me." My mother is not a fan of little girls in jeans or ponytails, and she doesn't seem to care that I hate wearing dresses. They're stupid, and I can't play in them. Though little girls aren't supposed to play. Or hang out with boys either, even if they are her brothers. I roll my eyes at the thought.

Linking my arm with Edi, I let him rush us out the back way of the palace, and I see Cade and Rohan across the greenery towards the edge of the trees. Edi rushes me towards them, as Erion jogs past us, laughing.

"Come on, slowpokes," Cade calls as Erion reaches them, but we're still nowhere close.

"You can run ahead, Edi. They don't look like they're feeling patient today."

"Emmy, no way. They'll just have to freaking wait."

"Edi, you cursed!"

"So what? People curse all the time at home." He shrugs but keeps us going, so I run to get there faster. I don't really like running, I always seem to trip over, but I know Edi won't let me fall. We run until we catch up to the others. Cade and Erion are the same age and have been best friends for as long as I can remember. They think we're too young for them to hang out with. Just because they're thirteen, they think they're so much better than us. Rohan is still a year younger than Edi and I, but I don't see why it makes a difference.

They're already walking off towards the waterfalls, so we follow behind with Rohan.

"Your mother cut your hair again?" I ask him quietly. His light hair isn't like his brother's or father's, and while his mother's hair isn't the shining ebony of Cade's or King Earon's, it's nowhere near as light as

Rohan's. It seems to get cut short every time his father gets angry.

"Yeah, Father got some bad news and lost it. He dragged me from the dinner table to my room by my hair, so Mother said it would be best to cut it. I was just starting to like it that long too," he pouts.

"Well, I think it suits you short." I smile at him, wanting to make him feel better.

"Your father is a dick," Edi snorts.

"Edi! Stop with the cursing!" I exclaim. He laughs at me but gives me a side hug then begins to climb the incline up the mountains to the top of the waterfalls. Almost no one goes up here, most people just swim in the lake at the bottom of the falls. But we learned last summer that because of who we are, it's easier for us to just go to the top to play. Rohan walks in front of me on the narrow path, while Edi stays behind me. Watching to make sure I don't fall behind or fall off, or something just as stupid.

When we reach the top, Cade and Erion are already messing around in the water, having stripped off because the blistering summer sun is scorching down on us all. I wipe the sweat beading on my forehead from the walk up, as Rohan and Edi both run off to join Cade and Erion in the water. They act like typical stupid boys splashing about and shouting, so I lay down near the edge of the waterfall and roll up the legs of my jeans. My pale complexion never changes, no matter how much time I spend in the sun, but I love the feeling of the sun on my skin. I close my eyes and listen to the sound of the water, which is almost loud enough to drown out the boys.

We stay out until the sun sets, and the night turns cold. Erion creates a fire for us to all sit around while the guys swap stories and I just sit and listen. Our parents won't care that we're still out, they never do. I just wish I controlled my fire as well as Erion and Edi… it never does what I want it to do. Father says I just need to focus more, that I'm too soft, not strong enough to wield it the way it needs. I need to learn to respect my powers, and then they will respect me and my wishes. I have no idea what he means, but that's all he ever says to me. So it's no real surprise I haven't exactly mastered it yet. My teachers don't help either. With basic academics, strategies, politics of our worlds, and histories I do great, but the physical stuff, defense, awakening your powers—that stuff I suck at.

"Girls can't fight in wars, don't be stupid," Rohan says to Erion, who was talking about a girl in his class who kicked everyone's butt except his.

"Rohan, you're too young to understand. This girl is a badass. She'd be a perfect queen. Full of grace, but deadly as any trained assassin," Erion says with a dreamy look on his face.

"Oooooh, Erion has a crush!" Edi laughs while Cade just sits quietly, looking into the flames. Erion and Rohan wrestle like they always do, I just laugh and shake my head watching them. Cade and Edi cheer them on, each rooting for their best friend rather than their brother. I stay sitting as they get closer to the edge, and I'm so busy worrying about them, I don't notice the noise behind me until I can feel the breath on the back of my legs.

I hear a low growl and turn, putting my back to the boys, bringing me face-to-face with five wolves, and I freeze. I know the worst thing I can do is run, but it's all I want to do. Except I'm stuck. I can't move a muscle.

"Help," I say, trying to shout, but all that comes out is little more than a whisper. I step back slowly as the wolves close in on me, my feet unsteady on the uneven ground.

"Emmy!" Edi shouts, but I don't dare take my eyes off of the wolves before me. I feel the fire before I see it, the heat intense as it flares past me, heading directly towards the leader of the pack. It hits its intended target, and two of the wolves immediately break off towards the new threat, while the remaining two stay focused on me. The leader of the pack is on fire as it runs towards the water. I hear growls and cries of the wolves as the guys try to reach me around the attacking pack. One wolf lunges towards me, but before it can bite me, something knocks me to the ground, and I hear Edi cry out.

I roll over to see Edi face down on the ground where I was just sitting, and the wolf's jaw clamped down on his shoulder as he screams. Cade uses his ice to send the other wolf running as Erion appears and uses his fire to scare this wolf into releasing Edi. A few more flares of flames from Erion and the pack flees back into the forest in the mountains.

"Holy fucking shit that hurts," Edi wheezes as blood streams down his top. I launch myself at him and wrap my arms around him.

"Thank you for saving me, Edi. I thought I was toast," I gasp as he winces. "Sorry! I didn't mean to hurt you."

"I'm fine, Emmy. I can feel it starting to heal already. I just feel a little woozy."

"You saved me," I whisper.

"I will always save you, Emmy. You're my twin," he says with a small smile.

"We should head back home," Erion says as he helps Edi up.

"You sure you're okay, Emmy?" Cade asks me as Erion leads Edi back down the mountain path.

"I am because of you and Edi. Thank you," I say, barely able to meet his eyes. My shame at not being able to save myself, for being too weak, mixes with the tingles of my crush for him and I feel myself blush. I hate that I'm not like everyone else, that I'm not strong like them. That I'm not powerful enough. My grandfather used to tell me I was going to be a useless Fae before he died, and I hate that he seems to have been right.

Emilia

Age 19

"Hey, Rohan, keep up! Otherwise, we're going to be late," Cade calls out behind us, as his little brother carries all of our things up the ridiculously steep hill to the Winter Palace. I feel a little sorry for him, but he'd never let me help him even if I offered to carry some of the bags.

"Why are we rushing, anyway? I hate these things, they're so barbaric," I complain, not for the first time. The King of the Winter Court, Earon Vasara, Cade and Rohan's father, is hosting the monthly 'party' that our two courts take a turn in hosting for the four Royal Courts. It's nothing but a brutal showing of power to the smaller courts and our people. It's disgusting, even if it is supposedly tamer now than during the war times. Though it seems to keep the peace during the cease-fire. Which is good considering the posturing that goes on while our fathers take their sweet time, supposedly working out terms of how to work together in peace, rather than slaughter each other. I'm sure more posturing goes on than any real peace talks because everyone wants what isn't theirs, and no one is ever willing to concede. It's a stupid fucking process, and one I know that Cade and Erion want to change when they ascend to their apparent thrones.

"Barbaric is the way of the Fae, sis. It's just in our nature. You never know, if you joined in you might like it." Erion, my eldest brother, smiles at me. I know he's trying to goad me, but he's not as bad as most of the Fae we know. And while he doesn't understand my aversion to our ways, or the disdain I have for the nature of our people, he's my big brother, and he'd defend me in even the worst of situations.

"Father agrees with me, well mostly." I stick my tongue out at him. "You must notice how he barely takes part in the games Earon puts on? He's only here because he has to be, just like he only throws these stupid parties for appearances' sake. It might be the one night a month when we let our darkest sides out to play, but not all of us have such darkness in us."

"I'm going to have to disagree, Em." I turn to Edimere, my twin. It's the strangest reflection when I look at him, but the similarities between us are uncanny. However, the surface is where our similarities end. I've never understood it, the darkness inside him, though I've never really tried. He's always been the cruelest of us all, and the thought of examining that too closely is enough to make me cold to the bone. It's as if the darkness torments and eats away at his very soul. "There is nothing better than the rush that comes from fighting for your life. It's like you're someone else. Or the feeling of power at holding someone else's life in your hands. It's a heady experience knowing you get to decide if someone lives or dies, watching them grasp at anything to stay alive, and watching that light die, knowing you did it. That feeling is indescribable. Father relishes in it, I've heard stories of his dalliances during the war times. He pretends not to like it for you, he holds back because he's afraid of what would happen if he let his beast out to play now that we're at peace."

I shiver at his words and notice the matching disturbed looks on Cade's and Erion's faces. Edimere is the other half of me, and I know he'd never intentionally hurt me—hell, he'd die for me, but he is definitely the darkest of us all, and he lives to see that darkness reflected in the people around him. He is of the Summer Court. Our people are cruel and brutal, but not usually so sadistic. The fact that Cade looks disturbed, and he is of the Winter Court—who are known for being sadistic, unfeeling, and cold—shows just how bad it's gotten. I worry about him, especially at events like this where depravity is encouraged and celebrated, but there is nothing I can say or do to change it.

Rohan catches us at the top of the stairs, panting and sweating as he drops the bags and cases to the ground. "I am so glad I get to skip this thing tonight," he grins with relief, I'm not the only one of us who is averse to the bloodshed for sport.

"It is the only bonus of being the youngest. I'm heading down to the square to party with a certain beautiful Summer villager, shh." He winks at me, and I can't help but laugh at him. Although dalliances between courts are forbidden, let alone a Royal with a commoner, he never seems to care too much. Rohan is more Summer than Winter. He's cheeky and carefree, mischievous and devilish, as free as a Royal not in line for the throne can be, and the rumors that the king isn't his father are just something we all ignore.

The creak of the door interrupts us, and I see Queen Lanora half smiling at us all congregated on the front step. "You are all late, the guests are going to arrive any minute. Get in here." We scurry inside at her terse tone, and I leave the boys to sort themselves. Grabbing my case containing the dress my mother picked for me this morning, I make a start towards my room. Cade stops me and takes the case from my hand as he smiles down at me.

"You don't have to do that, you know. I'm more than capable of dragging my bag with me." I try to take it back, but it's no use, so I just follow him down the halls.

"I know, but I want to help, so I'm helping." He smirks before continuing to lead me away from the entrance hall. He stops and looks over to make sure I'm still behind him, the smirk still on his face as he opens the door for me and waves me into my room. "After you, m'lady." I burst out laughing and shake my head.

"What the fuck," I say through my laughter, and he chuckles back at me. Light mirth isn't usually his way. His father is a cold and unfeeling man, and he's molded Cade in his image. Except for when he's with us, then it's as if he's a different person. His warmth and lightness fill me, and I try to stomp down on the giddiness I feel.

"It felt appropriate." His face darkens a little, and he takes a step closer to me, his eyes burning into mine as he brushes a strand of my hair behind my ear. "Stick close to me tonight. Edimere seems like he's getting worse, and I know how much you hate these things. He won't be able to shield you from it as he has in the past. I fear his darkness is starting to overwhelm him." My breath hitches at his touch. Cade Vasara has been the starring role in most of my dreams since I was a teenager, but he's Erion's best friend and the Prince of the Winter Court, heir apparent and next in line to the throne. So essentially, he's off-limits, what with me being the Princess of the Summer Court. I lose myself in the depths of his pale blue eyes, which are covered slightly by his shoulder-length, shiny ebony hair.

"You don't need to do that." The rasp of my voice gives me away, and I pull back. His eyes take in every inch of me, searing me with their heat before he snakes his arm around my waist and holds me in place. His breath on my skin gets warmer as he leans closer to me. I feel my eyes start to close, but force them open, not wanting to miss a second of our time together.

"Yo, Cade! Come on, man, we've got places to be," Erion's voice rings out down the hall. Cade steps back from me like I burned him and runs his hand through his hair.

"Shit," he hisses. "Yeah, yeah. I'm coming. No need to get your panties in a bunch," he yells to Erion, his voice more stable than it was a second ago. He turns to me, and I can't quite figure out the look he gives me. If it's longing or regret. I lean towards the latter, because well, it's him and it's me. "I'll see you in a few minutes, Em. Don't keep us waiting."

And in the same breath, he disappears from my sight.

What was that?

I try not to dwell as I throw open the case on the floor and turn to drop onto the bed when I come face-to-face with Ellia, one of the ladies' maids in the Winter Palace. She rushes me into the bathroom where she has drawn a bath, before insisting on helping me dress for tonight. I barely pay attention as she sweeps my long dark tresses into an updo and applies my makeup. I step into the black dress she holds for me. Combined with the heavy dark makeup and my dark hair, my pale skin almost glows in the dying light streaming through the windows. She kneels before me, fussing as I slide on the stilettos she's placed down for me just as a knock on the door sounds.

"Emilia, are you decent?" I look up and see Erion at the door.

"Hey, big brother, you clean up nice." I look at the black-on-black tux he's wearing, and like me, it makes his skin practically glow when paired with his dark hair.

"You don't exactly look like we dragged you hiking through the forest today," he says with a small grimace. "I don't think I like it." I pat his chest and laugh as I walk past him out of the room.

"This was all Ellia, she's a wonder. Shall we get going? The sooner we do, the sooner it's over."

"Maybe you should let loose Em? What's really the worst that could happen?" he asks, and I bite my tongue so as not to get into this argument again.

Instead, I sigh and place my arm through his waiting one, and let him escort me down to the ballroom while ignoring his ridiculous question. All you have to do is look at my twin to know what could happen. Edi wasn't always this way, he used to be so full of light and joy, a bit of a brute but he was a rogue at heart, now, you would never think those things of him. Just because I don't have that darkness in me now doesn't mean it couldn't be there if I followed the same path he walks down, and that isn't something I want for myself. I never have.

The shimmering gold doors of the ballroom sparkle in the warm firelight when they open, allowing us entry into the hellish event. The party has started without us, and I really don't mind. I look out across the room from the raised entryway and take in the garish decadence, defiled by the party's entertainment. Members of all the Royal Courts laugh and drink amongst the chaos and bloodletting.

I grab a drink from one of the practically nude servers as Erion grips my arm more firmly. "Well, it's not like this is our first time immersing ourselves in this debauchery, but it seems the king has gone all out tonight. The blood is already casting rivers through the room." His voice is quiet as it rumbles through his chest. He doesn't hate these things as much as I do, but he doesn't enjoy them like he wants people to believe either. Even with all of his bravado about me letting loose and embracing the baser parts of my nature.

The air in here even feels different from the rest of the world—the desperation from the helpless, combined with giddiness and bloodthirstiness from those in power. Erion guides me across the room, and I paint a cruel smile on my face to match my brother's, to blend into the room and avoid too many people stopping to greet us.

The biggest problem with being the Royals of the Summer Court is that everyone wants to greet us, regardless of how unwelcoming we appear. To be seen talking to Erion could mean power for a player on the board that is the Royal Courts. Women throw themselves at him, but he barely glances at them. None of this is anything new, I'm not sure why they continue to try with him. Socialites are not what my brother craves.

I tip back the glass and finish it in one go, placing it onto one of the many waiting trays around us. I step forward, but Erion pulls me back just as a young boy falls at my feet, blood spilling from his neck. I look down at his frail, pale body, and my heart clenches. He cannot be any older than me, if anything he looks much younger.

His eyes beg me for help, to save him from this fate. I step forward to reach for him when a cackle rings out around us as someone pounces on the body to finish their fun. I watch the woman as she straddles his waist, grinding against him as she laps at the cut on the boy's throat, her arms pinning his to the ground. My stomach turns, and I want to drag her off of him, but Erion holds me in place, stopping any intervention on my part.

The woman groans as she lifts her hands—each finger tipped with a metal claw—and slashes the boy's wrists, and she continues to writhe on him. She lets out a long, drawn-out groan as she tears the boy's chest open, and I feel my knees weaken as my stomach turns. Only Erion's grip on me keeps me standing.

"I'm just going to go get a drink and hide in a corner," I murmur quietly so that only he can hear. He releases my waist, but I feel his eyes on me as I finish weaving across the floor. It's as if I'm unseen when I am alone, despite being a Royal, which is why I hate being made to come here. Everyone wants to align themselves to the throne, ensnare one of my brothers into marrying them, but my gentler nature is not unnoticed. I am not seen as suitable or fit to be a Royal, though no one would dare to say these things in front of my brothers. The only upside is getting to spend time with Rohan and Cade. The five of us try to get away from it, the politics of it all, despite Cade and Erion being heirs to the thrones. It's stupid as far as we're concerned—the wars, the fighting, the distrust between the two courts.

All because about a couple thousand years ago, there was a betrayal between the two courts. Who was at fault depends who you ask, but essentially, the families crossed one another, and so the feud was born. It escalated to all-out war after one side—again depends which side you ask as to who was in the wrong—took the feud too far, and people ended up dead. Both sides said that the deaths would not stand, but no one would take responsibility for the deaths. That is, until my brother and Cade were born. My mother and the Queen of the Winter Court saw fit to align their husbands in a ceasefire for the good of their sons. Neither one wanted their son to be a target in a centuries-old war that no one really knew the truth of. I mean, I get it. It seems so stupid to hate someone just because of who their family is. If we can be friends, why can't everyone else just put this stupid centuries-old feud behind them? At least with the ceasefire, now it's easier, and maybe one day, when Erion and Cade hold the thrones, our world will look vastly different. Unfortunately for us, the Fae, while not immortal, are not that easy to kill without the right iron-tipped weapons. There are some illnesses our healers cannot mend, but beyond this, our cell regeneration from the power of the lands around us means we can live for hundreds, and in some cases, thousands of years.

I slide into a stall at the end of the bar and hide in the shadows of the corner. The server places a drink in front of me, Berripagne. I swear it's the only thing available at these things. I've grown to handle the tart taste and sharpness of the bubbles, but I don't think I'll ever enjoy it the way most people do. I sit and sip the never-ending stream of bubbles placed in front of me and pretend I'm anywhere but here. The hours pass and no one bothers me, it's bliss. I just imagine a land far from here, away from the darkness and stupid rules, while I try not to obsess about the fact that Cade nearly kissed me earlier.

"I thought I might find you hiding over here." Speak of the devil.

"You know me well, the shadows are always a good place to hide."

"Someone who looks as breathtaking as you do shouldn't be hiding in the shadows, Em." I don't know what to say to that, so I gulp down the rest of my glass. "Come, we should mingle with the masses, show our faces a little, and pretend that our fathers get on as well as we do."

"Can I not just leave? This entire night has been horrid," I say, but before he can answer me, I hear a roar —a pained scream.

"Rohan." Cade runs towards the noise, and I follow closely behind. The sight in front of me is enough to make me weep. I look at Edimere, covered in blood, to the girl at his feet, the life gone from her. Rohan is on his knees opposite the scene. I have no idea why he is here, he's not meant to be here.

"Why? Why her?" he wails at his father, who holds his shoulder and looks down disapprovingly as confusion covers Edi's face.

"This cease-fire is as fake as her professed love for you. She's a villager, and you are nobility. You shouldn't get so attached to them, Rohan. This was the best way I could show you the difference between them and us. Now the problem is solved."

"She never hurt anyone!" He shrugs off his father and struggles to his feet. Cade watches in front of me, trying to shield me, but I can feel how much he wants to go to his brother.

"She is a Summer commoner, you should not sully yourself in such ways. Next time, I will not be so lenient with my punishment. Plus, it looks like you could learn a thing from young Edimere. He is more Winter than you will ever be. I'm almost proud of the hand I had in his work this night," Earon boomed as Rohan's eyes grow dark.

"You did this!"

It feels like I'm watching in slow motion as Rohan picks up one of the many swords discarded around the room and runs towards Edimere, who meets him head on.

"You don't want to do this, Rohan," Edi shouts, meeting the sword blow for blow with the dagger in his hand, his weapon putting him at a disadvantage, but it's Rohan I fear for. I know my brother. I can see the darkness inside him taking over as the challenge intensifies. "I am not your enemy. I had no idea who she was, let alone that she was anyone to you. Do not make me do something we will both regret."

Edi's voice rings out across the room over the noise of clashing metal, while everyone just watches. The crowd cheers for the latest show of strength and the potential bloodshed. I gasp when Cade darts towards them as Rohan falls back to the floor, his white-silver hair coated in thick red blood, and Edi closes in on him.

I watch in horror as Edi raises the blade in his hand, his blue eyes now completely black. "I tried to warn you, Rohan. But you never listen."

I hear Erion shout Edi's name, but I'm rooted to the spot. I can't move. My vision blurs as Cade sweeps in behind Edi. At first, I think he's taken hold of him, but then Edi stops fighting and falls back onto Cade, who jumps back, looking down at the scene before him. That's when I notice the blood on Cade's hands, the iron-tipped sword clattering to his feet, and the red blooming on the chest of my twin's white tux. Chaos erupts, and I run to Edi, dropping to my knees, and place my hands on his chest.

"You're okay, Edi. I'm here. You're going to be okay," I say, but the blood coming from his mouth, and the fact that his deep-indigo eyes are glassy, tells me otherwise.

"Emilia, get out of the way!" My father rips me from Edi as the healers rush in. I look down at the blood on my shaking hands and back to my brother's now lifeless body. Erion crouches behind me, wrapping me in his arms as we mourn our loss together.

Cade stands with his brother and father on the edges of the scene. I feel Cade's eyes on me, begging me to understand, but the pain of losing my twin is too much, like half of my very being was just torn away. He steps towards me, faltering when his father places a hand on his shoulder. The conflict on his face is as clear as the tears that stream down mine.

"This is all your fault, you monster!" I scream at them, I don't know which one deserves it most, but it fits each of them. "I will never forgive you for this!"

My heart shatters into a thousand pieces, and I know that life will never be the same again.

1

I walk through the streets of Avaenora, the main city south of Eressea, where the Summer Palace looks down upon us all, with my head in the clouds.

To walk here, you would never know that we're at war. The birds sing, and people have stands out in the streets selling their goods, an array of spices, silks, foods and so much more, as they try to make a living in these trying times. The war has been hard on us all, and yet the people here still have hope that one day there will be a peace, and they will thrive again.

The sunbeams shine down upon us, and I can literally feel the rays rejuvenate me. Being part of the Summer Court, means that I have always had an affinity with the sun and fire. Strengthened because of my Royal lineage.

I watch on as I stroll through the city, as children run

and play around me, trying to keep their footing as they run on the gray and purple cobbled streets.

Excitement and anticipation flood me as I lose myself in the crowds of people gathering this morning, celebrating the new day. In the mass of people, I manage to lose the guard my father insists he doesn't have tracking me, but they are impossible to miss. His guards all carry themselves as if they have such purpose and look down at those around them. Apparently, being in my father's personal guard makes these men feel superior, despite the fact they're essentially on babysitting duty.

The hope of seeing Oberon fills me. He is the entire reason I made the decision to sneak out this morning. I know he's back from his latest hunt, one of many he's been sent on recently, and it feels like forever since he wrapped me up in the warm safety of his thick, muscular arms.

I remember the first time I met him four years ago as if it were yesterday. It was after one of Father's first, and probably most brutal, beatings. I'd finally figured out that my parents blamed me for everything that happened, and that nothing in my life was going to go back to normal. I was terrified having never experienced anything so violent towards me in my life.

And so, I ran.

I had nowhere to go, so I just ran and kept running until I ended up at the top of the waterfalls, where my brother had saved me once upon a time, so very long ago.

I curled into a ball and sobbed, finally grieving the loss of not just my brother, but of my parents too. They were never going to be my parents again, not like they once were, though the smallest sliver of hope still wrapped itself around my heart at the chance of maybe.

My mouth feels like I've swallowed sand. I stretch out from the ball I've been curled in for days while I've cried out every ounce of water in my body, or at least, that's how it feels. I've moved past the anger, past my idealistic denial of the things that have happened to me, and now that I'm past all of that, all I feel is numb.

Sitting on the edge of the cliff, my feet hanging over the drop, I stare out over Avaenora. I know now that its beauty is only skin-deep. That its beauty hides the true nature of this world and the people who live in it. Despite the beauty of our city, it holds the beasts that roam this world, encourages them to thrive. To live out their deepest and darkest desires, no matter how taboo or depraved they might be.

I'm so lost in thought, I don't notice the Hunters coming up behind me from the forest. You'd think I'd have learned my lesson in the past, but at this point, I'm not sure I care if they take me or not. The monsters run this world, and I am not one of them. I never will be.

"Well lookie what we have here, boys. A little lost

princess. I wonder what her daddy would think about her being up here all alone," the tall one at the front taunts as I scramble to my feet.

"Maybe her daddy doesn't need to know we found her. Looks like little Miss Royal upped and ran away. Nobody would know if we kept her for ourselves... or just played with her a little," the second jeers, as they gather around me, the cliff edge at my back. I stumble, and try to draw my fire, but not eating for days has left me weak. The flames answer my call, and the Hunters take a step back. They don't look afraid, just pissed off that I would dare to defend myself.

"You guys should leave, or it won't be my father you have to worry about," I say with as much strength as I can muster. My father hasn't taught me much, but how to draw on my strength in the worst of times, that's a valuable lesson to have learned.

"You stupid little bitch. You're going to regret threatening us," the third sneers. Their fingers morph to talons and I can't do anything but watch as the shadows swirl around them. These Hunters must be high in their order to call on the shadows the way they do, but I don't recognize them. Not from my father's guard, or from around the city, which must mean they're from the Winter Guard.

Fuck.

Hunters are shitty to deal with at the best of times, but any one from the Winter Court is no friend of mine.

They're brutal and viscous, even more so than the people here.

"You guys are a little far from home; you really should be heading back if you want to make it back in one piece," I snarl, refusing to back down. I don't know if it's brave or stupid, or if I really just don't care anymore.

"You should probably listen to the princess." I look behind them to see another Hunter, but this one I know. I've seen him around the palace more than once.

"Oh, fuck off, Oberon. You're not wanted or needed here," the first hunter says as he steps closer to me again, but I swear I can almost taste his fear. In a blink, he is lifted in front of my eyes, and his head rolls from his body. My stomach heaves as I try to process what is happening while Oberon stands there with a wicked smile on his face, the guy's head hanging from his fingers by his hair.

"Anybody else want to piss me off today?" he taunts, "Please, test me. I'm due a decent fight, and the two of you might just be enough to whet my appetite." He grins as he speaks, and the other two mutter under their breath before they slowly back away from me and disappear back into the forest.

At their retreat, Oberon throws the severed head over the edge of the cliff and kicks the body to follow it. "You shouldn't be out here alone, Princess. Especially at this time of night."

"Maybe I don't want to do what I should. And I'm not

alone, now am I?" I shrug but smile at him as I pull back the last dying parts of my flames. "Thank you for your help. I totally had it under control, though."

"Oh, you did, did you?" He laughs softly.

"Of course, I'm not just some damsel out here waiting to be rescued," I huff, my hands landing on my hips. "I can take care of myself."

"I can see that." He pauses and looks me over from head to toe and then back again. Shivers that I've never felt before run down my spine at his perusal. "I just thought I'd step in and save you the bother. Makes me feel good about myself. Being that guy, saving the girl. All white knight, you know the kind." He laughs again, and I can't help but laugh with him.

"But really, thank you." I step forward and put a hand on his arm. I've never really spoken to a Hunter before, they avoid me at court, but I've always been curious about them as a people. About their circumstances. How they deal with it all. "I'm Emilia, but my friends call me Emmy."

"I know who you are, Princess. We should get you home." I wince at his words.

"That place is not my home. Not anymore." I sigh. "But it's not as if I have anywhere else to go. My best friend is on the other side of the veil with her family, and everyone else is gone or dead. Oh my god, I sound like a whiny brat. I'm sorry, it's just been one of those weeks."

"Don't worry about it, Princess, I'm used to hearing

the Royals moan." He winks at me. "But we really should get you home. There have been people out searching for you since you didn't come home that first night. It is not fitting for the princess to be missing."

"Please call me Emmy, and I'm not missing, I was just trying to escape," I groan but walk towards him and follow beside him as he leads the way back to the palace.

"We all wish to escape at some time or another, but fate has plans for us all. Sometimes escaping is the exact opposite of what we need to be doing. Sometimes nothing can change unless we stay and fight against the wrongdoing and try to change it."

"It sounds like you've thought about this a lot."

"A man in my position has a lot of time to wonder about the cruel tricks of fate," he says, and nothing I can say won't sound like pity, so I say nothing at all. Somehow, the silence is comfortable, and we walk side by side until we reach the palace gates.

"Well, this is me." I point to the palace and laugh at my idiocy.

"I can see that." He smiles at me again, and with the warm light from the palace against the surrounding darkness, something about him calls to me.

"Thank you again," I say and reach up on my tiptoes and kiss him on the cheek. "Until next time."

"Until next time, Princess."

After that day, I sought him out, a friendly face in a sea of anger and indifference. After two years of being my friend, I gathered the courage to kiss him. He kissed me back with such passion that even the thought of it makes me sigh. Obviously, our friendship has always been a secret. A princess with a Hunter just would not do. I roll my eyes, practically hearing my mother's voice in my head.

Wandering these stalls in the morning, my face hidden by the hood on my black cape so as not to draw undue attention, is one of my favorite things to do. I can pretend the rest of the world doesn't exist. I don't feel the gaping hole in my chest from the loss of Edimere, my twin. I forget that my older brother has been gone since the day after Edi died, fighting the war with the rest of our soldiers against the Winter Court. I try to ignore the pressure from my father to marry into the Royal family of the Autumn Court to strengthen our position and our allegiance with them, and the fact that my mother will never speak up against him, no matter how unhappy I am, doesn't make my life any easier. Being a princess isn't as glamorous as everyone seems to think it is. I'd hang up my crown in a heartbeat for the chance of true love and happiness. Hell, I'd cross the veil into the mortal realm if I thought I'd ever truly be able to escape the reach of my father.

I weave through the crowds, tasting the foods from the traders and purchasing beautiful scents from the perfumers, hoping I'll get a glance of *him*. This right here is the life I've always wanted. To be just another person. There's nothing lonelier than being a Royal Fae. Being closed off from the world, it wasn't so bad before, when Erion and Edimere were here, but the only real company around the palace is my parents, the guards, or the Fae at court, and that is not the sort of company I'd ever choose to keep. I've never really fit in at court, I'm not quite brutal enough. I swear, the crueler you are, the better you do. People think I'm too soft, they expected me to raze the lands when my twin was killed, but rather than anger taking over, sadness did. Don't get me wrong, the anger is there, and it stays stoked within my heart, but I don't let it rule me. It's not like I'll ever forgive the ones responsible for his death, I won't ever have to, but I wouldn't flay the skin from their bones either. My twin was not well, his darkness was overcoming him, and he should have been detained, so that we could help him rather than slaughter him. Now I have to live with a piece of me missing—a piece of my soul was torn away. He was the yin to my yang, my balance, and for losing that alone, I will never be able to forgive the Winter Court.

I spot Oberon standing on the outskirts of the market square, and sigh at his dark beauty. I watch as he interacts with a little girl, she's too young to care what he is, and I laugh to myself as I watch him let down some of his walls and be silly with her. She hits him, and he falls to the floor howling in pain. I hear the girl's giggles from across the square, the sheer joy in a child's laughter is unmatched by anything else. He gets up and pretends to growl, and she squeals, pulling a face at him. I know just from this, that if it were possible, he'd make a great father one day. He, like me, is not like most of his kind, maybe that's why I love him the way that I do. Neither of us fit—both seen as outcasts despite the roles we're forced to play. I watch on as a frantic woman darts through the crowd and picks up the little girl, checking her over.

"Avalyn, what are you doing playing with this filthy animal?" she scolds the girl, setting her back on the ground. "Little girls do not play with Hunters!" I can hear the scorn and disgust in her words from where I stand, and I start towards them.

"As for you, how dare you interact with our children. You disgusting half-bloods are only good for one thing: cleaning up messes like the filth that you are. Don't you ever talk to my child again." She storms off, her daughter's hand in hers, spewing the ridiculousness of generations passed, and spreading it to the children. The look on Oberon's face will haunt me forever, he didn't choose to be what he is any more than I did, and it saddens me to see people avoid him, not even make eye contact with him, because of what he is. Something about the darkness within him, the very darkness I was once afraid of, calls to me and draws me in.

Maybe it's the Demon in him that people are afraid of. Maybe it's the fact that if the Hunters really wanted to, they could usurp the Fae Royalty and rule our world. God knows they're stronger than we are by far, and if it's even possible, more brutal. But because they are half-Demon, half-Fae, they're outcast and seen as beneath our kind, even though they work directly for the Royal families. They should be held in esteem, yet they're treated worse than the Elves that we love to hate. Unfortunately for the Hunters, their ancestors bound them to serve the Fae after a long a bloody battle, and an old magik holds them to their servitude, so unless they can find a way to break the bond, they must suffer the fate handed down to them. It makes no sense to me why they are treated so badly, but centuries-old grudges are what the Fae are best at, though personally, I've never really bought into the madness of it all. Maybe because I know what it's like to be cast aside. To be outcast by those who should be the ones you're closest to. The Fae are notoriously brutal with the truth. It's just in our nature, and while the Summer Court isn't exactly hugs and snuggles, at least we're not all as cold and unfeeling as the Winter Court.

I make my way over to him subtly, so as not to draw attention to either of us. While the Hunters work for the Royals, for me to be seen in public with one, alone… Well, the fallout would be seismic. One day, far from now, when we're far from here, none of it will matter. I hate that I can't be close to him, or be seen with him, just because of other people's sensibilities. It saddens me that his kind cannot cross the veil, because I have no doubt that with him by my side, over there, we could escape the pain and bindings of this place.

"Fancy seeing you here," I smile at him, and he treats me to a rare smile that lights up his entire face. I sigh at the dark beauty of him. It gets me every single time.

"Out here with the riffraff without your guard? Daddy won't be pleased," he teases, lifting his hand toward my hood, but catches himself before he touches me, and I can't help but feel a little deflated, despite knowing why he stopped. Loving someone is never easy, but loving someone who you're not meant to even interact with is so much harder, especially when everything has to be kept secret for fear of death.

"My father should know better than to put his goons on me. Despite his protests that he doesn't, they still try every morning to follow me. By now, I don't know why they even bother."

"Because despite your every wish, you're still Princess of the Summer Court, and you always will be."

"Forever is a long time, who knows what could happen," I say wistfully.

"You want to get away from all these people for a little while?" he asks, picking up on my mood.

"Where did you have in mind?" I say, letting my hand brush his, hidden by my cloak, and I feel him stiffen at the contact.

"You should be more cautious than you are, Emilia. You being hurt because of me would break me, and I don't think I could control myself if you were hurt. A lot of people would be in danger if I were in that sort of state. We shouldn't risk such things, I don't want to risk you."

"If people paid more attention, then maybe I would, but maybe, just for once, I want to be a little reckless. No one is going to see us. Just this once, for today, be reckless with me," I say, stepping closer to his huge frame and looking up into his yellow-gold eyes. The color gives away his heritage, they shine against the olive of his skin so beautifully. His face is unreadable except for the glow of his eyes, which he can't hide. I step a little closer, so we're almost touching, and I hear his breath pick up pace. "Take me away, Oberon."

He takes my hand and pulls me into him, I feel the air around us warp, and I know that he has hidden us from the world. His hand reaches up to my hood and pulls it back, revealing my long raven hair, which he runs his hand through. I grasp his thick biceps as I reach up to kiss him gently.

"I missed you too," he whispers as I feel the air around us shifting. The world outside blurs, but I don't care as he wraps his arms around me, and I feel safer than I have in a long time. He might be what the rest of my kind fear, but I know there's much worse at court than a Hunter. The subtle breeze around us stops, and I hesitate to step away. We get so little real time together, I want to hold onto this moment.

"We're here, Emilia." The roughness of his voice

touches each part of me, and I shiver despite the day's heat. I take a step back and pull away, his hand catching mine and holding as tightly as I do.

"Where are we?" I ask as I take in the beauty around us. The wonder on my face must be evident if the rare smile on his face is anything to go by. We're at the edge of the Eressea, and the sound of the waves crashing against the shore calms me. It's abandoned, with the remanence of a shipwreck in the distance, but not another soul around. I've never seen the sea before, the court is home, but it's also my own personal inescapable prison. We Royals don't really get to see the world other than through the memories of others. The fact that I get to experience this here for the first time with Oberon means everything, and I wish I had the words to tell him so.

"This is a place I found while I was out on my last hunt, and I knew you'd love it the moment I saw it. It's a small fishing town called Tamaya. I wanted to bring you here for a while, but it's so far away from the Court, I was worried that someone would notice your absence. Since you keep slinking away from your guard, I think we're safe here for an hour or so."

"Thank you, Oberon. It's so peaceful. I can almost pretend that the world back home doesn't exist, that it's nothing more than you and me."

"That could be our lives one day. We just need to plan carefully, but one day I'll take you away from there, and we can be happy. We can live long and peacefully. Just us and our family."

"You've got this all thought out, haven't you?" I tease as I shed my cloak and shoes, itching to move closer to the water. I can dream that our plan is all thought out, and we could run away tomorrow, but it would be just that. Dreaming.

"I have spent a lifetime alone, never thinking I'd find someone who accepted me for who and what I am, let alone someone that could love me. And never in that entire lifetime would I have imagined it could be someone like you. My kind doesn't find love often, you know that as well as I do. We're too unpredictable, the Demon part of us makes us dangerous. Unstable. We fuck and move on. I've only ever known one other of my kind find love, and that was with an Elven shifter. He left this life for her, moved to the Shadow Lands of Shani, and never looked back. I'd do the same for you in a heartbeat, Emilia. I just don't want you ever to regret our life."

I stand on tiptoes and kiss him with everything I have. "I have never and could never love anyone the way I love you. I wouldn't and never will regret a thing."

He lifts me and spins me around, his lips never leaving mine. I cling to him as he shrugs his jacket off and kicks off his shoes, removing my cloak before he runs towards the water. I squeal at the movement, and I hear him laugh. It's so rare that I quiet and enjoy it before he barrels us into the freezing-cold water, and I can't help but cry out in shock. My hold on him slips, but he holds me tight before submerging us both, taking my lips with his again. He lifts us, and we stay in the water, just messing around until the sun starts to sink in the sky, and my skin pimples with cold.

"We should probably head back," he says, pulling me towards the shore.

"Do we have to? I like seeing you like this. Can't we just run away now? Or at least stay away just a little longer?"

"I have somewhere we can go," he caves, and I squeak with joy.

"Thank you," I coo. I always hated those girls who acted crazy when they were in love, but these days I get it, and I just embrace the cheesiness that is my life when I'm with Oberon. It's the light in the darkness of my world, so I cling to it tightly. He wraps me up in my cloak and kneels, pulling on my shoes before dressing himself while I draw on the fire inside me to dry our clothes and heat us both.

"It's a shame that little trick of yours doesn't work in the water." He chuckles, shaking the water out of his shoulder-length dark hair before pulling it back and securing it at his nape with a leather throng.

"Water is a bitch for fire." I shrug and step into his embrace as he wraps us in shadow before traveling us back towards reality. We move in silence, neither one of us looking forward to going back. We stop sooner than I thought we would, and I look around in the darkness.

"Should we be here?" I ask him, looking at what I know is his home.

"Probably not, but I've not had enough of you yet, and I don't want to let you go." He kisses me brazenly, not caring who could see. I sink into him, forgetting the dangers around us.

"I don't want to go either," I whisper, and he pulls me towards his door, ushering me inside quickly.

His lips caress my neck before he pulls me backwards into the warm room. I hear the crackle of the fire, a comforting noise in the small house.

"This is beyond reckless, Oberon, what if someone saw us?" I breathe, turning to look him in the eyes, but he quiets me with another kiss and steals my breath, my worry fleeing along with it.

"No one would think to look for you here, Princess," he says as he nips down my neck and chest, making me cry out. "Why would someone like you be here with me? Our secret is safe here." I let his words wrap around me like a security blanket. I don't want to lose him, and that's what will happen if we're discovered before I have time to plan a way for us to escape this place. My thoughts evaporate as he unlaces the corset of my dress. He tears through the fabric and releases me from its confines before pulling it down to the floor, so I stand before him in nothing but my underwear and my black heels. I watch him as he seems to memorize the lines and curves of me.

"There are more reasons that I love you than in all of this life and the next, but looking at you right now reminds me just how much of a lucky son of a bitch I am." He smirks and rips off his shirt, and I see the faded white lines that etch his skin, a reminder that we are from two different worlds. Of the pain he suffered before he ended up here.

He stalks towards me, the predator in him gleaming in his eyes, and my breath catches when he reaches me and lifts me, wrapping my legs around his waist. Feeling him pressed up against me, knowing just how much he wants me turns me on so much more. I feel his sharp nails dig into the soft skin of my back, and I hiss when I feel wetness on my back where he broke the skin. He tosses me on the bed. The Demon in him is just under the surface, I can see the strain in him as he tries to hold it back. I sit up and motion for him to come closer.

"You want to play?" I taunt him, slapping his face before I run away from him, attempting to put some distance between us.

"You're playing a dangerous game, Princess," he growls as he crosses the distance in seconds, and his arms wrap around my torso. I shake in anticipation, knowing just how dangerous a game this is. Hunters are feared in our world, they are the punishers and the punished.

They're the big bad that goes bump in the night, more animal and instinct than anything else.

"Maybe I want to play dangerously, Oberon. Maybe I love that darkness that swirls inside of you. Maybe I secretly have a darkness inside me that matches yours," I say. I shudder as his hand works downwards and rips the black lace I wore especially for him from my pale skin, before rubbing the most sensitive part of me. I gasp as he bites my neck while he toys with me slowly, mixing pain in with the pleasure.

"I know you too well, Emilia. You couldn't handle the Demon in me."

"You won't know unless you try," I say as I tremble under his touch. He releases me from his hold and kisses down my back, kissing the punctured skin he created earlier, making me hiss.

"Don't push me, I don't want to hurt you." His breath is ragged as he tries to contain that part of him, the part I very much want to see.

"I don't think you could ever hurt me, I just want to be with you. All of you." He lifts each leg and removes my shoes then sweeps me back up into his arms, his black hair in his eyes, unable to hide the glow of them—the yellow-gold giving away his true nature.

"Don't try to run from me, and I'll give you everything you want."

"All I want is this. You. Us." I sigh, my breathing stuttered by the closeness of him.

His lips crush mine, silencing my words, the world around me disappears, and there is nothing but him. I feel his muscles tighten when he lies me down in front of him on the bed.

"First, let me love you, then I'll show you who I really am."

"Promises, promises."

I hear the boom a second after Oberon, who leaps from me and morphs into full-blown Hunter mode, as he protects the door between us and whatever is trying to get in. The thunderous noise of heavy footsteps clambering up the wooden steps towards us fills my ears as I cover myself with the blankets on the bed. I want to step forward and help, but I know that few things can come through that door and best a Hunter. The door explodes inward, and I feel the splinters from the door fly past me, some embedded in my skin, but I don't feel it. All I feel is fear for Oberon as I see who stands on the other side of the door, and I hear Oberon roar as he tries to shield me from the opening with his body.

"I suggest you put some clothes on Emilia and call off your beast," my father's voice booms around the room, and I want to shrink inside myself. *Why did we come back here? We should have just gone somewhere far away and never come back.*

I feel more than see Oberon leap forward as my father's guards attempt to enter the room. The screams curdle my blood as he defends both his territory and me. I hear the shots I know will be from my father's guards and cry out as Oberon drops to the floor. I scurry over to him, not caring who sees me.

"Emilia, for goodness sake, cover yourself, or I will drag you back to the palace naked for all to see," my father roars. I grab my dress and throw it on myself, my eyes barely leaving Oberon. "It was just a potion to knock him out, he's not dead," my father says, but it doesn't help me breathe any easier. I know the punishment that will await Oberon for having me here. For loving me. I stop the tears from falling and stand tall, my chin held high.

"What are you doing here, Father?" I demand as his guards tie Oberon's wrists and ankles.

"I got wind of your whereabouts. After your disappearing act this morning, I had people out looking. Imagine my disgust when I heard you were with this… animal." The hatred and loathing pour from my father's face. "Take him to the cages," he orders, and his guards lift him despite my protests.

"I will never forgive you for this," I swear to him.

"Emilia, you were a disappointment long ago, long before you decided to debase yourself with this filth. At this point, you should just be thankful you're not joining him." He spits at me before turning and walking away from me. I watch as the guards take Oberon away. Another guard enters the room and grabs my arm to the point of bruising.

"Sleeping with filth like that. Maybe I'll have my way

with you too, and then let the boys have you. I'm sure after that beast, you'll even enjoy it. It doesn't sound like your father will mind if you come back a little worse for wear," the guard sneers. I put my hand on his face, channeling my fire, and take joy in his screams as his skin bubbles beneath my touch before he falls to the floor as my fire takes him.

"Maybe you should remember who you are talking to," I tell him as I step over his writhing body. I extinguish the flames and walk away, back to the palace, back to my prison.

I enter the palace that is my prison. It has been my entire life, though more so the last few years. The cold emptiness of the palace just screams death and darkness, from the dark stone walls to the black marble floor. The only light is from the scones on the walls, casting a warm but dim light causing long shadows. I see my father pacing in the entrance hall, my mother quietly standing in the corner like the good wife she's always strived to be. Unfortunately for me, being a good wife apparently means being a lousy mother.

"I see you ditched your guard yet again," my father booms as he barrels towards me, his hand raised. He strikes my cheek hard enough that my knees buckle and send me to the floor. I hit him with a hard look as I try to ignore the agony in my jaw and notice my mother hasn't moved or made a sound, not that I'd expect anything less at this point.

I gather myself and stand in front of him, because showing weakness in these walls is not an option. "Yes, well, when your guard threatens to rape me and then let his friends do what they please to me afterwards, I figured I'd show him the repercussions of his revolting actions. Considering he's one of yours, I shouldn't have been surprised," I snarl, the bite in my voice hits its target, and my father lashes out again. This time I stay standing and prepare myself for his long-standing form of punishment.

"It should have been you that died that day. Your brother was worth so much more than you. He at least understood his place in this family. Your allegiance was more to the Winter Court because of that murderer than to your family, and now you embarrass us further by cavorting with Hunter filth. My guards could and should have done with you as they wanted, maybe then you'd have realized just how far you've fallen. You're a disgrace to our name, to our family. You are less than worthless." The words pierce the armor I learned to put up a long time ago, but the guilt from the fact that I'm still here and Edimere isn't, it haunts me daily. I've always known my parents blamed me, but they've never said anything quite so direct as this.

"Well, I'm glad he's not here to witness this. He would be ashamed of who you have become since he died. He'd have gone against you for hitting me too, and you know it, but I guess I'm not the only one tarnishing his memory, am I?"

A roar escapes him as he attacks me again. I zone out as I fall to the floor, and he showers me with his anger. The kicks are the most brutal, and I wish I could say this was the first time. I hear his pants, the exertion getting to him as he leans down and places cuffs on my wrists, I see the runes cut into them along with the bright green stones and know what's coming before I feel it.

"Let's see how quickly you forget your place this time without your powers to help you heal." The venom in his voice doesn't escape me. "Maybe next time you want to dishonor our family by sleeping with animals, you'll think better."

"My entire family are animals, it's not a surprise I fell in love with one," I force out. Just breathing hurts as I feel my strength drain thanks to the cuffs.

"Take her to her room and lock the doors. Do not leave the door unsupervised unless on my order. She wants to cavort with filth, she'll be treated as if she's nothing better than the filth she claims to love." He signals to the guards who are placed around the room. I grew up with these people watching out for me, and not one person says a word. I groan as I'm lifted, and the pain in my body is highlighted with each step taken towards my rooms. I hear the creak of the door open, before feeling softness below me.

"I'm sorry," I hear softly before my door closes, but think nothing of it as the world fades to darkness around me.

I peel one of my eyes open, the other too swollen to open. The light that shines through the windows makes me wince and jolts my body. The sharp movement makes my entire body ache, the pain stealing my breath. I lay back down and try to catch my breath as the night before slowly filters back through my mind, and I'm filled with a different kind of pain.

Oberon.

I wouldn't wish the cages on anyone, and I can't imagine what it's doing to the Demon in him, being confined in such a small space, and that's if he's not in chains.

I try to sit up, but the pain shoots down my arms, and I hear the clink of my latest accessory. Elven cuffs. The best way to render a Fae powerless and essentially human. The power that runs through my blood is extinguished, meaning that I can't heal my broken bones, I can't defend myself, and I also have absolutely no chance to escape. I try to climb out of bed, but my legs don't have the strength, so I fall and groan once again as my body takes on further damage. Struggling into a sitting position of sorts, I notice the new bars on my windows. As if the cuffs weren't enough, the entire room is a magical dead zone. Freaking wonderful.

The door opens briefly, and one of the girls from the kitchen scurries in, placing a tray on the table on the other side of the room, before opening my voile curtains, letting in more light and making the bed, all while ignoring me in a pile on the floor. She leaves without acknowledging my existence. I guess the loose friendships I had with people around here aren't as strong as their fear of my father. I can't really blame them considering how he treats me, I wouldn't wish this on anyone.

I struggle over to the table, assessing my injuries as I go. Without my powers, this is going to take weeks to heal fully. I slowly lift the lid on the tray and let the aromas fill my senses, a nice distraction from my current situation. I lift my fork to my mouth and try to savor the flavors, but my pain and worry for Oberon cloud everything.

My father's temper is legendary, and really, what he's done to me is nothing. Just the tip of the sword for him. But with Oberon locked away, fully subdued, and at my father's mercy, I don't want to imagine just how creative he could get. All because I asked Oberon to be reckless for just one day. I never imagined that us just being us for a day could end this way. We're usually so careful at his insistence, but I was tired of only having stolen moments. I wanted more. I guess you really should be careful what you wish for.

2

lose track of how long it's been since I was locked away in this room, but I'm starting to lose my mind. I know that it's been at least two weeks because most of my bruising has gone down, and the only real pain I have left now is more just discomfort from my ribs, but the loneliness makes it feels as if it's been at least six. I look in the mirror in my bathroom, the only one that has escaped my frustration thus far, and see the toll of being separated from my magik. I have cried and shouted, pled and begged at the doors for someone to let me out, to help me or at least just talk to me. I got so angry at one point that I destroyed what I could of the room with my waning strength and my injuries, but all that happened was they came in and wordlessly fixed things or removed them, just adding to my desperation.

My thick and shiny hair is limp and lifeless, and my

skin has lost its healthy glow. I only know it's nearing the end of the day because the sun is low in the sky. I miss it's heat on my skin, the wind in my hair. My kind is not meant to be separated from nature, not like this. We are of the earth, it feeds the essence of who we are. Even with the cuffs, the outdoors would've helped.

I've not interacted with anyone since my father ordered I be locked away, despite trying to talk to the people coming in and out of the room and the guards on the other side of the locked door.

I hear the door to my room open, and at this point, I don't even bother to pay attention to whoever it is. I'm sure it's just my dinner being delivered. Just another wordless face passing by, forced by my father to treat me like I barely exist.

"Emilia?" The voice echoes through my rooms, and I wonder if I've actually lost my mind to the point of hearing voices inside my head. I make my way back to my bedroom and see my mother's handmaid, Trestella, standing at the end of my bed.

"Emilia, look at you. What a mess." Her disapproving look just pisses me off.

"Yes, well. It's not like I asked to be beaten and have my powers taken away," I say with snark, how dare she.

"Don't you take that tone with me, young lady, your father is hard, but I'm sure you deserved every part of your punishment. Disgracing your family like that, as if they haven't been through enough. Ungrateful little bitch.

However, despite my personal feelings about your lack of punishment, your parents have asked me to remove the cuffs and prepare you for dinner, so that is what I will do."

"I'm not hungry," I protest. It's stupid, but I'm so sick of my life being ruled by other people's wishes. No matter how much I want these cuffs gone, I can't stop my rebellion at the orders.

"Stop being an ungrateful little brat. If you're not hungry, don't eat, but you are still going downstairs." She reaches forward and grabs my ribs, which still ache, and squeezes to reinforce how powerless I am against her. She laughs as I try not to show my pain before she unclasps the cuffs that have bound my powers. I hear the noise at my windows of the bars being removed, and relief floods me. I can get out. As soon as they're gone, I feel my power coming back to me, like a long-lost friend. My fingers and toes tingle as the sensations come back. The trickle of power fills me slowly as if it knows I'm fragile from being cut off for so long. I feel its warmth as it fills me, healing me as it reaches my broken and aching parts. I contentedly sigh once I feel fully connected again and pray never to be cut off from the earth again for as long as I exist. "Now, go get yourself cleaned up and presentable. I'll be waiting outside to escort you down to the dining room."

I look down at the silk shorts and camisole I'm wearing, they're pretty gross at this point, but in my defense, I had no real idea how much time was passing, and I slept a lot to keep the pain and loneliness at bay.

"I want to know where Oberon is. How he is." I don't care if I'm acting like a petulant child, after being locked up in here with nothing but my thoughts for company, I need information.

"And I want to be able to magik money in the world, so I don't have to put up with your shit, but wants don't get us anywhere, so I suggest you get a move on before I drag you downstairs as you are," she spits at me before spinning on her heel and leaving the room, slamming the door behind her.

I turn and head back to the bathroom, normally she wouldn't dare to speak to me in such a way, but apparently, my parents have made it obvious to the household that I am not of any importance, and so it's free reign. I turn on the shower and undress in seconds. I let the scalding hot water beat down over me, letting it invigorate my body along with my powers, which are almost at full capacity. I feel the hum of them under my skin, a feeling I don't normally pay attention to, but one I've missed dearly. I shut off the shower and reach deep into myself and finish healing the broken ribs from my father's heavy swings.

I dry and dress quickly in the long black dress that is hanging in here, I'm sure courtesy of Trestella. Despite not wanting to see my parents, I want information. I finish touching up my face in the mirror, adding some kohl to line my eyes and a deep red to my lips before presenting myself before the ogre that waits for me. I open the door to my room to find Trestella waiting for me, she looks me up and down, then with a small, sharp nod of approval she starts walking down the hall, obviously expecting me to follow, so I do. I don't want to ruffle more feathers than I need to, even if she is a raging bitch. The guards and other members of the household refuse to meet my eyes as I walk down the hall. I straighten my back and raise my chin, I will not let them see how broken I've felt, though I've no doubt they heard me at my weakest. I refuse to be that person again, and for now, they will only see what I let them.

I follow her to the small, private dining room my parents favor when they're not entertaining the rest of court. My parents are both sitting at the long, dark table, and my father motions for me to sit to his right, so I do. The tension in the room is thick, despite the insincere smiles on their faces. I don't trust those smiles, they're almost creepy. Smug even. I am shocked, however, to find that we are not alone. At the table sits my father's most trusted and closest friend and his wife.

"I trust you're feeling better," my mother says, clasping her hands in front of her. Her acting could win awards

"Oh yes, I'm splendid." I can't help the sarcasm that overrides whatever politeness they expected as I find the strength not to roll my eyes.

"Emilia, you will watch your tone." My father slams his hand on the table, startling Mother. I guess the pretense isn't going to last long after all.

"Or what, you'll beat me and send me to my room again? How original."

"No, but I will punish your lover further." He chuckles, sending shivers down my spine. "He's hard to make scream, but the sound is exquisite once it happens." A dark smile graces his face, and any appetite I may have had disappears at the news of Oberon. Apparently, his friends know of my situation, not that I'm surprised. They probably helped him come up with more creative ways to elicit screams.

"You need to release him, he has done nothing wrong but love me," I demand, only just managing to keep the quiver from my voice.

"I do not need to do anything, and you are not in a position to barter here." I take a deep breath so as not to lash out. Usually, my anger is non-existent, at most, a low simmer, but not here, and not now. Not with this.

Dinner is brought out to the table, and conversation skips to idle chatter about the courts and the gossip that is the lifeblood for my mother and her gaggle of bloodthirsty friends. My presence is no longer noted, so I sit quietly and shove the tasteless food down my throat. All I can think of is Oberon and what my father might have done to him. I need to get him out, so I spend the rest of the meal plotting, trying to come up with a way to free him rather than pay attention to the monotonous talk of torture and who did what better than who around me.

When dessert is taken away, my father's friends stand and say their goodbyes, and my mother escorts them out, leaving the two of us in a long and painful silence. I want nothing more than to leave this room and try to work out how to fix this mess I've gotten us into. We wait until my mother returns, and to my surprise, rather than my father standing to leave, my mother sits back down opposite me, refusing to look at me. I look towards my father, who looks disgustingly pleased with himself, like a cat who caught a bird and devoured it, and a flood of apprehension fills me.

"Did you enjoy your meal, Emilia?" His smirk prods me, and I'm sick of playing nice. He's up to something, I just know it.

"What do you really want, Father? I know you have no care for whether I enjoyed myself or not." I know there's more to this. He looks too happy, and not just because he's taking pleasure in my discomfort.

"You have missed some very important news recently while you've been out gallivanting, but a treaty has finally been agreed in the last few weeks between the courts. The war is going to end, we will resume the cease-fire, and your older brother can finally come home." I gasp at the news. The courts have been fighting longer than I care to think of, and Erion has been gone since the day after Edimere was killed.

"Erion can come home? I don't understand…" My eyes bounce between my parents. It doesn't make sense.

"There are conditions to the treaty. For the courts to truly be at peace, we must come together with a joint goal. Earon and I have decided the best way to do this is a joining of the courts, and the Kings of Autumn and Spring are in agreement. Everyone is tired of wartimes." It takes me a moment to understand, but then it dawns on me.

"A marriage?" I already know the answer, but I want them to say it.

"Yes." My father nods, and my mother's eyes stay downward, not looking at me. I stare at her, hoping for some sort of clue.

"I don't understand what this has to do with me. Surely Princess Araya of the Autumn Court will marry Prince Cade, and it is done. They are aligned, and it makes the most sense." The Autumn Court has always aligned itself with Winter, as the Spring has aligned with us.

"Not quite." The glee on my father's face makes sense. Dread fills me, and I feel paralyzed until my anger breathes life back into me.

"I will not, and you, above all others, know why. How could you ask me to marry the man who killed Edimere? We shared a womb, came into this fucked-up world together, I will not marry the monster that took him away from me!" My shouts echo around the room, but my parents stay seated, unfazed.

"You will if you want your animal to live. King Earon

has decided that the three Royal Courts shall put forward candidates of Royal blood to win the prince's heart, and the one he picks shall be his wife, giving whichever family he picks a new height of power. For you and the Winter Prince to be wed could mean no war ever again. The Autumn Court is already too close to the Winter Court. Strategically it gives us no advantage." His words trickle out, and everything makes sense. "And just to add an incentive, to make sure you are selected, if you fail in winning the prince's favor, I will kill your Hunter. Slowly. And I will make you watch. So, you can see the results of your actions, and he will know that you failed him. More importantly, you will know you failed him. Either way, I win."

My stomach drops, and I swallow to stop the rising bile. I wish he wasn't serious, but I know he is. It's the perfect plan for a man like my father, and the glee on his face leaves no room for interpretation of his feelings about it all. I will suffer either way, but if I am successful, he gets his favorite child and heir back out of the line of danger, and if I fail, he gets to torture Oberon and me for however long he sees fit. I cough as the bile rises again, and I fight it as my father watches on, the smug look on his face makes me want to burn it off.

"Mother, you cannot let him do this. I am your daughter! You can't think that this is fair or a good idea. THAT MONSTER KILLED MY BROTHER!" I feel the tears run down my face as my mother dismisses me.

"Your father is a brilliant man. If he thinks this is for the best, then we must do as he wishes." Her voice is weak and timid, and for the umpteenth time, I wonder who she would've been if Edimere were still here. If she hadn't married my father.

"This is insane. Cade will never believe that I would choose to marry him. We may have been friends once upon a time, but times have changed and so have I. With others to choose between, there is no way he is going to pick me."

"Well, I suggest you work it out," my father says as he stands, my mother following his lead. "You have three days to get something together because that's when you leave for the Winter Court." He starts to leave the room, my mother scurries behind him, and I swear to myself to never become the person she is.

"WHAT IS WRONG WITH YOU?" My voice screeches in my desperation. "Where is the man who acted like my father? The man who picked me up when I fell and told me to follow my dreams and my heart, no matter the cost. Where is the man who was my hero? The man who would slay any demon for his children."

He spins on his heel, and the burning hatred in his eyes breaks me all over again.

"That man died the day Edimere did. And again, the next day when Erion left us because of it. All I was left with was you, an ungrateful, pathetic, spoiled little whore. You could have stopped it, stopped Cade from killing my boy. Every time I look at you, all I see is everything I lost, and I can't stand to look at you. My boys were my heirs, they were strong, fearless, and above all else, loyal, and while Edimere had his cruel streak, he was still a great man. You are nothing like them, you never were. That's what happened to me. You happened." He spits on the floor, making sure I know just how little he thinks of me, before storming out of the room. I hear the slamming and crashing, followed by screams as my father's anger befalls the house again.

I catch my head in my hands and let my tears fall onto the dark shine of the table. I didn't think my father could hurt me deep down, not anymore. Not more than he already had. The shock of his words isn't enough to numb the wounds he caused, and the ones he reopened. I fear this has been coming for a long time, a way for him to punish me for what he blames me for, and now he just has the perfect circumstance. I have no idea what to do. I do not want to be the cause of Oberon's death, but there is no way I will convince Cade that I *want* to be his wife.

Fuck.

After Father's meltdown, my presence is ignored throughout the palace. At the same time, everyone takes cover from the overflow of his anger, and I take the opportunity and escape to my last safe place; to my best friend Lily's. Her home has been my sanctuary more than once, and sometimes I come down to the stream behind her house even if she's not here.

"What did they do now?" she asks as she sees me approaching from her seat beside the flowing water. She stands, worry etched across her features. I lose the strength I've been holding on to, and let down all my walls, throwing myself into her open arms, we fall back to the grassy ground. I open the dam of emotion that I've been holding back, spilling every detail.

"I get that this is a shitty situation, Emmy, but Cade Vasara isn't exactly a bad catch. I know how much you hate him, and I wish I could do something to help or stop it, but we both know your father. And we both know he won't hesitate to kill Oberon. What your father is doing is diabolical—no two ways about it—but considering it's him, it could be worse. He could have just killed Oberon and still forced you to do what he wants. We both know he has ways of making you do what he wants. He's a vile, despicable asshole, but he's manipulative as fuck and knows how to get what he wants. I don't want you to do this, I wish you could be happy. I want nothing else for you. I just don't see any other way," she says, sadness tinging her words. She lies back onto the grassy verge beside me, staring up at the stars. I sigh and stare up at the vast darkness, wishing I could focus on how beautiful the sight is. Lily might be the person who knows me the best in the entire world, but her taste in men is beyond bad.

"He killed my brother, and there is no way in this reality or the next he's going to believe I actually *want* to be his wife. He knows how I feel about him, and if he doesn't, he's a fool. I'm pretty sure most of the courts know how I feel. No one is going to be expecting me to be there, it's a joke. All I want is to find a way to get Oberon free and get away from here." I get up and dip my feet in the stream, cooling down.

"Not to play the devil's advocate here, because your dad might as well be a goddamn Demon, but you're not getting Oberon out of the cages if your father has him locked down. He's a devious asshole, but he's a clever one. No one has ever, in the entire history of our race, escaped the cages. As much as I love you, you can't do this. You'll get yourself killed, which would kill Oberon too. Marrying Cade would be easier. It means that everyone gets to live. I'm sure Oberon would understand, he knows your father. We could try to get word to him somehow. It's a shitty path, but it's the one of least resistance, I guess. The easy option is to do as your father asks. I wish I had a better option for you."

I lay back down beside her. Realistically, I know she's right. Even if I had a plan, I'm not the hero type. I'm not physically strong, well not compared to the guards at the cages, and plotting an escape isn't exactly in my repertoire, but I don't want to give in and give up hope.

"Again, that depends on your definition of easy. He killed Edi. All over some stupid lesson King Earon was trying to teach Rohan. It broke the cease-fire for fuck's sake. I'll never forget the look on Edi's face when Cade betrayed him. When Cade's blade pierced his heart. Edi wouldn't have really hurt Rohan, I believe that."

"Fae are a fickle kind, we're rash and passionate, but cruel and brutal. Sometimes these are our greatest powers, sometimes they're our biggest weaknesses. Have you ever considered what would've happened if Edi had killed Rohan? You guys are Royals, but so is Rohan. Edi likely would've been killed anyway if he had killed Rohan, so they'd both be gone. We all know the only reason Cade wasn't killed is because he's the heir. Plus, this whole insane thing affected everyone, not just you guys. The cease-fire was broken, the war restarted, and hundreds of lives have been lost to the war in the last few years. Hell, that's how you lost Erion because his anger got the better of him and because he is a Lieutenant of our armies. He ran off to avenge his brother in the only way he knew how. I get that what happened was awful, but what I'm saying is that it's not a simple as you make it out to be. Have you spoken to Cade since? It's been over five years, and you were all so close before it. The five of you were inseparable, and one day, one moment, one act, blew it all to hell. I understand your pain, Em, but sometimes you need to let stuff go before it swallows you whole. I say this as your friend because I hate to see you holding on to so much anger and pain, but you held your grudge against Cade and Rohan when it was their father who orchestrated the whole thing. Anyone can see that he plays with them like he does the rest of his court. The boys were merely just pawns in yet another of his twisted games. You should think about it—talking to and forgiving Cade, I mean. Maybe he feels guilty, regret even."

"Of course, I haven't spoken to him, and if it weren't for this ridiculousness of my father's, I wouldn't ever have to. And why would you even suggest it wasn't his fault? Nobody made him pick up that sword and kill my brother. The circumstances are irrelevant. I can't believe you're saying all of this after all this time," I cry out in frustration. "I hate feeling so fucking helpless, so trapped. I also hate being so fucking whiny, why couldn't my father just leave me alone. God knows he has plenty of outlets for his anger."

"Ah, yes, I heard you guys are hosting again tonight."

"Oh, the delights." I roll my eyes. You'd think that considering everything that happened, my father would hate those horrific monthly parties, but no. Now he revels in them despite the tension it adds to our lands, even if he thinks it boosts the spirits of our people. "But seriously, Lily, what am I going to do?"

"You're going to suck it up, that's what you're going to do. If you love Oberon as much as you say you do, you'll make this sacrifice for him."

"Do you have any idea how tormenting it is to both love and hate someone at the same time? Especially when the reason you hate them is now a gaping hole inside your chest. I loved Cade, even if it was stupid, young, puppy love, but regardless, I loved him, and then in an instant, he broke me. His actions tore my world apart, and I could do nothing but hate him. Those emotions warred for years, and now, when I'm finally in a place where I can be happy, my jackass of a father does this to me. I don't want to see Cade again, I don't want to have to deal with that conflict. I buried it with Edimere, and that's where it stayed. Deep and buried and in the past."

"Hey, I'm not saying it doesn't suck, it definitely does, but you're a grown-ass woman now. You can handle Cade Vasara and his cute ass. Just because you hate him doesn't mean you stopped loving him. It's a fine line to walk, you know." She laughs, and I push her over, making her laugh more.

"You're so much help!" I roll my eyes and lay next to her.

"That's why you love me. But seriously, imagine if you could stop the wars, stop the barbaric parties. Our entire world would be transformed."

The sound of my heels bouncing off the walls of the corridors is the only thing I hear as I walk towards my mother's day-rooms, and try to temper the nerves that feel like they're going to shatter me into a thousand pieces. The silence is a stark reminder of just how empty this place is now that my brothers are gone, there's no life here anymore. I hear the soft sound of violins as I get closer to the room, it sounds so heartbreaking, so haunting, but so beautiful all at the same time. My mother's soft voice sounds as she sings to the melody. I don't remember the last time I heard her sing. Maybe this will go better than I hoped. I push down the sickness that threatens to overwhelm me with a small amount of hope that this might solve all of my problems. This is my last chance, my only hope.

"Mother?" I knock once, peek through the door, and see her standing on the balcony. She visibly startles from my presence before she stiffens and enters the room.

"What are you doing here, Emilia?" My shoulders drop at the change in her, and the hope I had dwindles to almost nothing.

"I came to ask for your help." I take a few more steps into the room. It's been so long since I was in here, I've not been welcome anywhere near here since Edi died. "I know how much losing Edi broke you, and I know how much Father holds over you, but I'm still your only daughter. Please help me reason with Father. This madness isn't going to fix anything for anyone."

"You stupid, selfish little girl!" The sting from her hand on my face knocks me backwards, and pain shoots up my spine from colliding with the door handle.

"What the hell!" I cradle my face, I can't believe she hit me.

"You come in here like you've done nothing wrong and ask me for my help, saying it's not going to fix anything. YOU'RE THE REASON THIS IS ALL HAPPENING! If you'd kept hold of Cade that day, he never would've killed Edimere. Erion wouldn't have left us. We wouldn't be at war. WE WOULD BE HAPPY! But no, you just stood there like a stupid fool, and then cried when it happened. Because you did nothing, Erion left. Now you can finally redeem yourself a little and bring him back, and you ask me to change your father's mind? Are you insane? You were practically in love with the Vasara boy once, I'm sure you can fake it again. God only knows you followed him around like a pathetic lovesick child before."

I have no words. I knew my parents blamed me, but for my mother to lay it all out like that... I turn on my heel and rush out of the room, not stopping the tears as they fall, I don't stop until I reach my room. I've been subjected to my mother's silver tongue before, but she's never been so brutal. So direct. There was no love left in her eyes for me. I thought she was weak and feeble in front of my father, scared of his wrath, but now I know the truth of it. She truly blames me. I knew my father did, but I never knew why. Now I do. My revelation hits me—I truly have no one left at all.

I sit and cry for the loss—for my brothers, for my family, for Oberon, and for a chance at love in the future. I can't let Oberon die because I wanted a chance to be reckless, and if I can bring Erion home, then I will. Even if my parents still hate me. Maybe I'll get to see him again. We haven't seen him since the day he left, with only sporadic letters to let us know he is still alive. If I can change this for him, then I will. I have to.

3

*M*usic hums through the room, dulling out some of the whimpers and groans imprinting their agony into my soul as I smile and play the role expected of me.

I pluck a glass of Berripagne from the tray as the server walks past me at the latest monstrosity of my father's imagination. He's having a party—if you can call it that. I sit on the outskirts, using the burn of the alcohol to make this scene bearable, as I watch the debauchery of the upper-class Fae delighting in and bathing in the pain of the lower classes and the humans kidnapped from beyond the veil—the forced entertainment for tonight's show. This is the reason I do not belong here. I take no pleasure in the pain of others, which makes me barely one of our kind if you ask the people here.

I watch as those with the upper hand clap and squeal

in glee, covered in their finery and jewels as they watch those not as fortunate. Both Fae and the human fight, bleed, and die before they, quite literally, bathe in the blood of the combatants, getting off on the death and the power they hold.

My eyes cast to the thrashing of naked skin on skin, two bodies writhing together as they fuck in a bath filled with the blood of their kill, the tortured lifeless body still in there with them. Deep cuts decorating her once perfect flesh. She's been shredded until her veins drained every drop from her, her lifeless eyes stare wide open at me and a shiver races up my spine. What a waste of a life. The worst part is that that's not even the worst thing happening here. Gut-curdling screams echo from thick black curtained partitions, causing my stomach to coil. My instincts are to go to their aid, stop this sadistic fucking shit once and for all and teach the people of the court, these sadistic bastards, a lesson in compassion and decency. It's not our way, however, and I can't intervene and live free to tell about it.

Am I one of them if I just observe? If my body is in this room, but my soul, my heart is in those baths, behind the curtains with the victims of circumstance? No matter how much I tell myself I'm forced to be here, it won't stop the memories and terror keeping me awake at night. I'll never be able to burn these images from my mind.

I wouldn't be here if I wasn't forced to be, but I can try and think of how to save Oberon, whatever the setting.

Just because I'm here physically, doesn't mean I condone or take pleasure in such brutality or that I have to be present mentally.

One part of me, the part stuck on the dilemma I still have to work on, knows that if I were queen, I could help the lower classes. It would take time, and I'd never be able to stop it completely, but I would have more power to try. More power to do something—anything.

Right now, I can do nothing but sip my Berripagne, let the buzz chase away the deflation of my soul, and just stare at the walls so that my absence isn't noticed. Not that I'm sure it would be. I'm pretty sure demanding my presence here, making me wear this ridiculously heavy dress that blinds me each time the light bounces off the gems on the corset, is just another form of punishment. Tonight would be the perfect time to try and break into the cages to free Oberon, most of the security has been pulled here for the event, to keep the unwilling participants in line, at my father's decree.

He never used to be this way. Be this man. But it's hard to marry up the man he was to the one before me. I seek him out amongst the throng of bodies moving and grinding with each other. A slither of disgust and guilt crawls through the marrow of my bones as I witness him holding a girl not much older than me by the throat, his long fingers cradling her life with such ease in his grasp. The curling of his lip opens up a pit within me as he turns her small frame and shoves her forward into one of the large baths laid out throughout the hellish room. Her blonde hair becomes swallowed by the crimson flood of blood as she disappears beneath its fury. Her slender frame begins to convulse, her hands splash and struggle as my father delights in the poor undeserving girl's battle, making her choke and swallow the thick liquid, restricting her oxygen until she can't take it anymore. Her fight begins to flee, and her limbs become limp before he pulls her free. A red waterfall streams down her face as she gasps to fill her burning lungs. Just when her chest settles from heaving, he plunges her back into the depths of the tub. I wilt on the inside, he's not just killing her, he's killing me, the child inside me that calls him Father. What sort of sickness is this? My mother stands beside him, her tall stance proud and inspired. She's wiping the blood drops that have spattered over his face like she's cleaning a child's face after dinner.

The escapism of it all isn't lost me, the rush of power they feel, knowing how much control they have in their hands.

Life and death, pain and pleasure, mercy or condemnation. It's all in their hands. And by the look on my father's face, he gains a heady rush from such things. It's almost foreign to me after the man I thought I knew. Seeing the remorseless horror at the hands of the Winter Court Fae was one thing, but this... Shit like this party is why Edimere died, the revelry in brutality and pain, and it's why I avoid these things as much as possible.

"Emilia, come here." I jolt from my frozen spot where I'd been standing for the last ten minutes. My mother's voice is spoken with a shrill ring inside my mind. I hate that she can get inside my head, while I build my walls to stop people prying around in my thoughts, I've never been able to block her from projecting her thoughts into my head. I look back to the women who gave me life, and swallow the dregs in my glass to stop my throat from closing up. I want to ignore the request, but her eyes tell me before her voice returns in my head that she wants me to go to them right away, and she better not have to ask twice.

Willing my legs to move, I take tentative steps in their direction. Weaving through the gathering of people, I try not to slip on the blood spilled on the ground in the ridiculous stilettos my mother picked out along with this dress.

Muscles pull taut in my shoulders as I reach them, and I see a spark ignite in my father's eyes at the sight of me.

"Come and join in with the festivities, child. You look like someone soured your drink," my father bellows with a hard chuckle. The crowd that surrounds him cackle as their eyes focus on me.

I school my features to mask my burning anger and revolution at his flippant remark of what exactly this party is. It's a bloodbath, not a festivity of any kind. He can call it a celebration if he wants, but it's nothing more than death and carnage, pain and cruelty.

"I'd rather not ruin my manicure." The words slip from my lips with ease, my hand lifting to wave my fingers at him. The excuse came to me on the spot, vanity over the barbaric activities would be believable amongst such a crowd.

"Nonsense," he booms. A tug of his lip forming a wicked smirk. "I won't hear of it, and you can get your nails fixed tomorrow if you really need to. Now, come take this one from me and let loose a little," he demands, thrusting forward the blood-soaked girl in my direction without releasing her. I look at the girl, and it scares me how much she looks like me, despite her hair. It's like he's killing me in the only way he can get away with, and now he wants me to kill myself instead. His games never fail to shock me, but this… A lead weight pools in the bottom of my stomach at what he's inadvertently telling me.

I look around, and all eyes are on me observing, goading, adding pressure I don't want or need. The tightening of my chest crushes down on my heart as I paint a smile on my face so they can't see that I'm trying not to run, to evaporate into the air and become invisible to them so I don't have to do something I won't be able to live with after. Pressure pushes down on me as I feel the weight of hands grasp my shoulder. My head turns briefly to see one of my father's friends looming over me.

"Come on, child, live a little." He takes a knife from his chest pocket, dried blood already crusted on the tip, and forces it into my shaking hand. "If you've never tried it, how do you know you won't like it. The Winter scum deserve your wrath, don't you agree?" he teases.

And it's those words that speak to the inner voice whispering inside me. It's what terrifies me more than any of this. What if I was just like them? Just like him and these people I loathe. I don't want to be like them. I try not to question why my father has Fae from the Winter Court here despite his newest treaty, as much as I want to distract myself from this moment.

Steadying my trembling hand, I curl my fingers around the handle of the blade and close my eyes as they all laugh at me again. I don't want to do this. They all know that and they're feeding on my discomfort, reveling in my reluctance and fear for their own gains. Regardless of my feelings towards the Winter Royals, their court does not deserve my wrath, despite my parents' beliefs.

Their excitement and menacing cheers scrape at my sanity, threatening to break me.

I stumble forward when my father grasps my wrist with his bloody hand and yanks me towards him, where he still holds the poor girl by the back of the neck. Her legs are barely keeping her upright. I think if he let go, she'd crumple to the floor in a heap, and I may dissolve with her.

"Show us who you really are, Emilia. I know it's part of you deep down, you just need to taste it, and you'll never turn back," he taunts. I flash a look, pleading for mercy to my mother, but she turns her face from mine, leaving me cold and empty. The lump clogging up my throat makes it hard to speak. All I can hear are my father's words as the blood rushes through me, I step towards her, and she whimpers, flinching slightly, at least I hope it's her.

"Oh, just get on with it," a female voice chimes in, and I see Natalia smirking at me over my shoulder as she marches towards me. This crazy bitch has hated me my entire life, but she loved Edimere more than life itself, so I never made my feelings about her known. They were well suited. She was as cruel as he was, it was as if they were developing their cruelty together. But since he died, she's continued the journey they were on. She's been crueler and more twisted than ever. More than I thought possible. Her manic grin is way too close for comfort and despite my usual speed, I don't have the power to stop her.

My world slows, the atmosphere thickening with a suffocating fog of despair. I can't react, it's too late, my eyes see, but my mind has taken a back seat, leaving me with zero ability to prevent her from grasping my hand. She rams my arm forward, plunging the blade through skin, muscle, and bone of the young girl's throat. Wide, shocked blue eyes burn into my own as the life and light fade from the girl's face. Blood spurts from her like she's a broken faucet on a sink, coating me in my sin, my unwilling deed. Her murder.

Screams rattle around my body and bounce around the

space in my mind. I search for who they belong to, but it's me. The screams are my own.

If it weren't for my wails being drowned out by the cheers around me, the celebration of me taking a life, they would have angered my father, but he's too busy joining in the round of applause.

My hand loosens its hold on the blade, and the room rushes into focus around me as the girl's body is released from my father's grip. She thuds to the floor like nothing more than a lump of slaughtered meat. I battle to comprehend what's happened, what I was forced to do, what *she* made me become. Natalia, grins at me, blood coating her hand from the squirt of the severed artery she caused using my hand as her weapon.

"You had no fucking right," I croak out, my hand swinging at her face, but she's fast, faster than me at least, and anticipates my reaction. Her cold, callous fingers grab hold of my offending hand. She doesn't realize her mistake though, all I feel is a burning rage growing, building. I don't think, all I do is feel as I release the pain and anger inside me, reaching for my power, my fire. I unleash it on the room with a fury like no other, starting with Natalia. I pay no mind to her cries as the anger courses through me gaining momentum and wrath.

How fucking dare they make me do this, and then cheer in the sight of my misery and regret.

My heart thunders in my chest as the power races through the very fabric of my being. I watch as the fire coming from me ignites the clothing of those closest to me, engulfing them in my wrath, my justice. The only people not trying to flee are those who are designed like me, and who feel nothing from the fire I'm raging into the room. A scream tears from me, causing the flames to leap higher. I never wanted to be this person, they coaxed the darkness from me, and now are coated within it. This entire night is disgusting, and I want to scorch it all from my memory, and from my sight, from the world. I no longer care about the loss of life, just as they all wanted.

A force from behind me shoves into me, sending me tumbling to the ground with them on top of me. I'm consumed by the weight of whoever is pinning me beneath them, as they put a stop to the destruction of all the things I hate.

"Get off of me!" I bark, struggling to shift the weight on my back. Suddenly a sense of dread fills me as an icy cold rush of magik kills my flames, filling me with a cold essence.

The weight moves off of me, and I turn to sit up, faced with my father's smug face and another who causes a gasp to leave my lips.

"Nice to see you again, Emilia." The familiar voice deepens the ice already seeping into my blood, freezing my veins.

"Rohan," I whisper, a shiver racking through me. "Why are you here?"

"I'm saving the day it appears. That's quite a temper

you have." He smirks at me, and the cold is gone. My anger returns with dull force, and my blood boils as I stare at Cade Vasara's younger brother.

"Why are you here?" I grit out this time with more bite.

"I'm here for you, obviously."

4

I pace my room while Rohan sits on a chair by the window in silence. I don't speak. I can't. How dare he be here. In my room. Summoning me to the Winter Palace! I thought I had more time than this. I'm not ready. The shock from what just happened clings to me. This is all too much at once.

"Are you okay?" Rohan stands and moves towards me, but I step back and try to breathe. "Jesus, Em, sit down before you fall down."

I do as he says, but more so that I can curl up and steady my breathing.

"Only my friends call me, Em, Rohan. You don't get to call me that anymore," I tell him once I feel more like myself, he looks like I just hit him.

"I get that. Sorry." He seems more composed and so

far from the boy I used to know. "I'm assuming no one told you I was coming?"

"You assume correctly. They even told me I had more time than this to prepare."

"It seems a lot has changed." He shakes his head and runs his hand through his long white hair.

"More than you could possibly imagine." I sigh as I start pulling clothes from my closet and throwing them in the open trunks that have been brought up.

"Considering what I walked in on, I'm going to agree with you. I have to say, I was shocked when they told me that I'd be coming to get you. All things considered, I figured you would be the last person on the planet to want this."

"You and me both, buddy," I mutter.

"Sorry, what?" He looks at me like I've got two heads. Apparently, my new learned sarcasm isn't something that will be welcomed brightly at Winter Court.

"Nothing, I just mean that I was surprised by the treaty. If I can be a part of bringing Erion back home, bringing home all of those pour souls fighting out there for a fight that isn't their own, just to have enough to feed their families, then I want to be a part of that." I'm not lying, but it's not the entire truth either. I do want everyone to come home, I just wish there was another way.

"I'm sorry, Emilia." I turn to look at him, and the remorse on his face is apparent. "Everything got so out of hand that night. I was irrational, and not completely in my right mind. I overreacted and played right into my father's evil games. I know that it was more about his boredom and hunger for war than it was about stopping my dalliances. There's nothing I can say or do to change what happened to Edimere, but I want you to know how sorry I am. I do not expect you to forgive me, though, I hope you can. We've tried to reach out over the years, Cade and I, but we weren't surprised when we didn't hear back from you." I'm not sure how to take that, I had no idea. He might be sorry, but it doesn't change anything. If it wasn't for that night, I wouldn't be here right now, so I say nothing and finish packing up the belongings I'll be taking with me.

I walk down the stairs to the main entrance hall with Rohan on my heels and find my parents waiting for us, my father's shirt and hands still stained with the blood of his victims. I try not to think about what he made me do— what they made me do. I don't want to lose my stomach or my control. I keep my head high as I approach them. I refuse to let them see the anguish I feel inside about being cast out of my home, even one as ghastly as this.

"A Vasara at your heels, Emilia, how fitting. It's almost like they didn't take everything from us already and you've just gone right back to how things used to be.

Rohan dear, you always did have a sweet spot for our daughter, isn't that right?" My mother sneers as if she's smiling. Her words land where they mean to as I see Rohan's face turn red.

"How dare you speak to me like that, Galadriel. Let us not forget why I'm here, and who begged who for this opportunity. You should mind your tongue before you lose it. I'd have thought Oisin would have kept you better in line." Rohan stands tall, retaliating against my mother's wretched words while reprimanding my father. I watch as she shrinks back behind my father, and his face turns a strange shade of purple.

"You two should leave now, before I lose my temper. Remember your place Emilia, and don't you dare disappoint us." He turns on his heel, and drags my mother back down the hall to the ballroom where his guests are no doubt waiting for him to continue in their torture games.

"I'm sorry, Rohan. You didn't deserve that. My parents are just... Well, you might have noticed that they've changed since you last saw them." I try to be civil, to wash the shame from my parents' behavior from me, and I hate the words as they fall from my mouth, my bitterness squeezing my heart.

"Don't you dare apologize to me for them, Emilia. You've never really been like the rest of your family, and while you might think they've changed, they haven't. You just never really saw their true nature before. You have no need to apologize to me. Now or ever." He nods at me and lifts his arm, motioning to the door, and escorts me out to the horse-drawn carriage waiting outside.

"I thought you'd appreciate this more than walking all the way like the old days. It's a long way. Plus, we must go the long route because while the cease-fire has been reinstated, the lands of war are still mainly full of soldiers along the border. I've made sure it's fitted with extra blankets and such, what with the cold seasons creeping in the north. You never did much like the cold."

"Thank you, that was very thoughtful of you," I tell him as he opens the door and offers me a hand into the carriage. I have no idea what is going to happen over the next few weeks, but I take a deep breath and steel myself against it all. I don't get to be Emilia, the girl who lost her brother and loves a Hunter. What they'll get from me is a mask—all they'll see is Emilia, the girl who wants to forgive and forget, the girl who wants to make things better for the courts, a girl willing to sacrifice for the greater good. If they knew the truth, they wouldn't let me through the front doors.

5

*I*t's as if no time has passed at all in Ringa. Once we passed the war-torn lands at the borders, everything looks exactly the same through the valleys and the towns. The carriage turns a corner to the long winding entry of the Winter Palace, and anxiety floods me at what is to come. I focus on steadying my breathing, being back here brings it all back—the good and the bad—and it's as bad as I feared it might be. I shake the sleep from my limbs and stretch out as much as I can in the small space. We traveled through the night, and thankfully, I managed to sleep most of the way, despite the severe drop in temperature once we crossed the border into the Winter Territory.

The sunlight makes my eyes sting, but I welcome its greeting, even if it does make the palace look majestic as it glints off the white and gold beauty. It almost looks as if it's made from ice, which seems only fitting. The memories of my childhood and everything I once had assault my mind, and I try to focus on anything but them, the laughter, the friendships, the tears.

"Are you okay?" Rohan's voice filters through the fog in my mind and brings me back to my unwanted reality

"Not exactly somewhere I thought I'd be again, it's just…" I take a deep breath as my heart squeezes, thinking briefly on everything that could have been.

"Painful?" he asks, and I nod. He sends me a small smile like he understands my pain. It occurs to me that it couldn't have been easy for him to come and get me. To come to our home, knowing everything that happened, what was set in motion by his actions. To see what monsters my parents have become. To feel some sort of responsibility for it all, and I soften to him a little. He didn't have to come and get me himself, he could've sent anyone. But if he's anything like the Rohan I used to know, there's no way he'd have made me face coming back here without a familiar face. Without someone who knows just how hard this is for me, no matter what I say or how much I pretend I'm fine. I guess, despite all of the changes at home, not much has really changed here.

"There's a lot of history for you here, it's why we, other than my father, were so surprised to see your name on the list, or a submission from your court at all. I'm pretty sure I was the only one who took it at face value, the others, well they might not have missed you like I did." He nudges me with his shoulder and smiles. His words give me little comfort. I can't say I didn't miss him, for a while all I did was miss the way we all were, the ways things used to be, but I don't think I'll ever forget that he was at the center of everything that came to be. My emotions are a tornado, swirling inside me so much I don't know which way is up. I mask my face and paint on a smile to hide the turmoil and conflict I feel inside. I might not be ready for any of this, but I'm sure as hell not going to let anyone else know that.

"I appreciate the warning. When are the others arriving?" I ask, trying to change the subject.

"They're already here. They have been for a few days. Cade and my mother weren't convinced about you coming here for the right reasons, or if it was even remotely a good idea, but as always, Father had the last word, and so you're here." He shrugs, and I get it. They don't trust me or want me here. Just another obstacle to overcome.

Lucky me.

We pull up in front of the steps that lead to the main doors, and I freeze. The last time I stood here, I was so carefree. Hell, the last time I stood here, I had a massive crush on Cade. These were the only people who accepted me, who didn't judge me for being who I was. Even more so than my brothers. Even being from Winter, they didn't ever seem as cold and brutal as I had been taught to believe. So much time has passed, so many things have changed. But Oberon needs me to do this. Erion needs me to do this. I take another deep breath and climb out of the carriage, putting my hand in Rohan's waiting one.

"I guess we should get you settled," he says, tucking my hand into the crook of his elbow. I might not have forgiven him, but I'm willing to lean on him right now, even if just a little. Time to fake it till I make it.

I follow his lead and ascend the steps to the doors which sweep open before we reach the top. The chatter in the rooms fills the air, along with laughter, and the chink of cutlery on china. As we reach the top, I see a foray of people, rushing around, glasses and plates of food being dashed into what I can only assume is still the small dining room. A voice calls out to Rohan from the room, and with a sigh, he leads me towards the room and the voices. Squeezing my hand quickly, he releases me and puts some distance between us before we enter. A hush descends over the dining room at our arrival.

'No need to stop on our behalf." Rohan saunters over to the table and grabs a handful of bacon, stuffing it in his face. "Come on, Emilia, looks like they saved us some space up here."

I watch from the doorway as he moves towards the head of the table where Cade is seated, with two empty seats to his right.

Just wonderful.

I adjust my smile and follow him through the room, sitting when he pulls out my chair and assess the room. Opposite Rohan is a man I don't know, and he eyes me with the same suspicion I instantly feel towards him. I can't put my finger on what it is, but everything about him sets off alarm bells internally. The other four seats at the table are filled with princesses from the other courts' Royal families, and surprisingly Araya isn't here. I file a mental note to ask Rohan why later. The petite redhead with unnaturally blue eyes sitting next to me is Centra Samhradh, and next to her, her elder sister Yasmina, the Princesses of Spring Court, who could be twins. Talia Natsu and Arabella Verano, cousins to Princess Araya of Autumn Court are the youngest ones here. They complete the awkward table, they all seem to be pretending to be friends, hell they might even *be* friends. I wouldn't know because I avoid as many court functions as I can, so it's been more than a while since I saw anyone but Araya. What I do know is that something like this, essentially fighting for the same man, they will be lucky if their friendships survive.

"Safe journey, brother?" Cade asks Rohan as he sips his coffee. I feel the heat on my skin as his eyes land on me, and I cannot help but look. Our gaze locks and it's as if the room falls away. The connection I always felt is there, and that hurts more than I'm willing to acknowledge. He tears his eyes from mine, anger painted over his features before he schools them back to the pompous asshole look he had before, and my anger shrouds me again like an old friend.

"As expected. Gave us some time to catch up." Rohan

smiles at me as I reach for the coffee pot, and I don't miss the skeptical look on Cade's face. I guess I'm going to have to work even harder than I thought if I'm going to convince him I want to be here, even if Rohan is seemingly on my team for now.

"It was lovely, thank you for sending the carriage. We would've been here sooner, but I didn't realize when Rohan would be arriving, so I was a little behind. Glad to see everyone else here made it on time, and apologies again for arriving so much later than everyone else." I speak through my smile as Rohan tries to hide his laughter. Everyone here knows why I'm so much later than the others, but I'm not going to let that get in the way of saving Oberon's life. That's why I'm really here. Not for their games. Not to fall in love with Cade and have a happily ever after, and especially not to make any friends. Despite what they may think of me, they don't really know me at all. I may have to give up my life and my happiness, to soothe the soul of my wicked father and be a pawn in his games, but I'm not going to let any of them know that.

I lift the coffee cup to my lips and try not to sigh at how good it smells after sleeping in the carriage, but I dare not eat. The bile swirling in my stomach at being in the same room as Cade threatens to overwhelm me. Sickness and hatred war inside me, but you'd never know it to look at me. In the last few years of my life, I learned how to wear a mask, to not show weakness. To not wear my heart on my sleeve. What happened the last time I was here changed the course of my life. I didn't get to be that carefree girl anymore. I lost all of my friends and my family in one moment. Because of what happened here. Because my father's torture has been merciless and never-ending as a result.

Lily might think I should blame King Earon the most, and while I do blame him, the king didn't put that blade in Cade's hand. I still believe he could've prevented what happened in a different way, any way but that.

Conversation picks back up around me, and I realize I've been lost inside my head, but I keep myself quiet, assessing what is essentially my competition. I may not want to be here, but here I am, and I'll be damned if they think I'm going to lose this sick game.

After what feels like a lifetime of idle chatter, Cade stands, commanding the attention of the room. I've not really let myself focus on him since I sat down, instead, paying attention to the women of the room, but now I can't help but take him in. His dark hair is just as I remember, but his eyes are just as telling, and he is not happy.

"Ladies, please excuse me, I have things that require my attention. Rohan and Lex will be around if you have any questions, but as you're aware, my mother would like to speak to each of you alone this morning too. Please make yourselves comfortable. For as long as you're here, my home is your home." He leaves the room, and he is every bit the man I remember, but not all at the same time. His tall, strong frame and obvious muscles are accentuated by his white button-down, even causal as he wears it with the arms rolled up. His hair is just as shaggy as it used to be, and I try not to ogle his tight ass covered by the tight black trousers as he leaves. I might not like him, but I'm not blind, and I'd have to be to not be affected by the sight of him. This man is a stranger to me, and any advantage I thought I might've had with knowing who he was, disappears. The boy I once knew definitely isn't here anymore.

"You want me to show you where you're staying?" Rohan leans over, half-eaten apple in his hand, his white hair getting in his eyes.

"Do you ever stop eating?" I laugh and shake my head. "But, sure. Lead the way." He stands and pulls out the chair for me as I rise. I nod to Lex, a goodbye of sorts, but he scowls at me as Rohan escorts me from the room.

"Who is Lex?" My curiosity gets the better of me, and I can't help but ask.

"Lex is Cade's newest leech. Sorry, friend. His closest confidant and General in the Winter Armies, though he spends more time at Cade's side than on the battlefield where he belongs. Rumor has it that he is half-Elven, he's an evil little bastard so it wouldn't surprise me. He worked his way up from sewer rat in the last five years to now being the right-hand of the heir to the throne, and I couldn't trust him less if I tried." I laugh, it's weird that it almost feels like nothing happened, like that day didn't happen, when I speak to Rohan. It's as if I'm the girl I used to be, rather than who I am, and while having a friend in him would be nice, especially if all goes according to my father's plan and I'm here forever, I still can't lose the wall between us. It would be too easy to lose myself in the process.

"You're not a fan?"

"Nah, Lex's a snake, he seems to have everyone else fooled, but I see the real him. He doesn't try to impress me, and why would he? I'm just Cade's younger brother. I can't help him step up in our world. I'm not sure exactly what his angle is, but I know he has one. One day I'm going to work it out and have him banished from Rivinea."

"So, don't trust him. Got it." I realize where he's led me to, and I feel the blood drain from my face as he opens the door in front of me. "My old room," I whisper. I falter as I start to step through the door and end up sitting upon the bed in the center of the room.

"I thought it would be nice for you to have something familiar since you were back here, in what essentially is a snake pit. Everything considered. I'm sorry if I was wrong." Rohan strides towards me, stopping just short of arms distance.

"It's fine. I just didn't think..." My voice sounds raw, barely more than a whisper as I battle the lump in my throat. The last time I was in this room was the last time I was truly happy. I swallow, trying to keep a hold of the emotions threatening to overwhelm me.

"I'm going to let you get settled." Rohan squeezes my arm and offers a small smile. "If you need me, I'll be in the library, not much has changed, so you'll find me easily enough. Mother will want to see you at some point today, but I have a feeling she'll save you for last."

I nod and watch as he walks away, shutting the door behind him, before turning and facing the room again. Climbing further back onto the bed, I wrap my arms around me.

I might not be able to do this. Not even for Oberon.

I knew this was going to be hard. Being here. Being around them. It's exactly why my father wanted me here. To punish me. To torture me. If I could have found a way to save Oberon and get Erion back without being here, I'd have taken it. But now I'm here, and I'm in this situation, helpless. I can't do anything but try to get through this, to do what my father wants me to do. I fall back onto the bed and let my tears fall. It's been a long time since I've cried, but right now, I couldn't hold them back if I tried. I can't even put my finger on what I'm crying for. Mourning for Edimere. Mourning for the loss of a life and love with Oberon. For the chance that I might save Erion from having to continue to fight this war. Or the fact that I'm essentially giving up any chance of happiness and love to free the ones I love the most. It could even be the fact that I have to pretend I've forgiven the ones who hurt me the deepest, to play another role, hide the horrors their actions created. I have to not be who I am, potentially for the rest of my life.

I look up at the sound of the knock on my door as it opens slowly.

"Cade." I wipe away my tears and try to mask the mess that is my face. He steps into the room, his movements stunted as if his body rebels against the action. I tense as he comes towards me, my conflicting emotions whirling inside of me fighting for dominance, and I flinch when he nears me, causing him to stop his approach.

"Emilia, are you sure you want to be here?" he asks, and the sincerity in his voice threatens the tears I've just put a stop to. Gone is the man from breakfast, and I catch a glimpse of the boy I used to know. I feel myself weaken against him, but then a flash of memory from my last night here hits me, and I steel myself against it.

"Of course, the room, it was just a shock, that's all. Being back here is all just a bit overwhelming. I didn't think I would be this emotional." I grind the words out as I twist the truth, and I can't tell if he believes it or not.

"I can understand that. The last time you were here, well, it was all just a fucking mess in honesty." He scrubs his hand down his face as he looks around the room uncomfortably. There's not really much I can say to that, and this whole thing just feels really awkward. I get up and step towards him, trying not to let my true feelings filter through, to reassure him, but his words stop my movement.

"Though, if your brother had shown better self-control, maybe we wouldn't be where we are right now." His cold and unfeeling voice is like a bucket of ice water to my face, a full one-eighty to his words a minute ago, and I grind my teeth not to say something I know I shouldn't. "I'm not surprised you put yourself forward. It's definitely one way to try and apologize for the mess your family created that day."

"My father thought it would be a good idea," I respond between gritted teeth. How fucking dare he try to blame my brother! "My mother agreed, and so did I. It's our responsibility to bridge the gap between our courts, especially considering the events that ended the cease-fire in the first place." The politeness of my words is like a hot pin in my stomach. "If we can find peace between us considering our history, then our people should have no problem believing that the peace between the courts is achievable. The past is the past, and that is where it should stay." The words burn on my tongue, the lies, the half-truths. He eyes me like he doesn't quite believe my saccharine words, and I can't really blame him. He knows me, or at least he did, and he knows just how much my brothers mean to me, so he'll also know just how much everything that day broke me. He just won't have any idea how bad things have gotten at home. No one outside of the household truly knows, apart from Rohan now, I guess.

"As long as you're happy, Emilia. That's all I ever wanted for you. Good luck with Mother today. Maybe we can catch up properly soon?" I nod, trying to keep up with his dual personalities as he bounces between them so easily, and he leaves the doorway without a second glance. He's just as cold and unfeeling as his nature wants me to believe he is, despite the small lapses of personality, but for all I know, this is who Cade is now. Maybe he's not who I remember. I don't believe anything he said, and I refrain from trying to find meaning in his words. All he ever wanted, yeah, right. The fake sincerity shone through, despite my heart wanting to believe it was the truth. Why even come to see me if he was just going to lie to my face?

It might be hypocritical considering my position here, but I have no choice, he didn't need to come here. I stand and close the door, creating a false sense of privacy, but one I need. In here, I can almost pretend that nothing ever happened, but it will also be a good reminder of why I'm really here. My newest prison.

I walk through the empty halls of the Winter palace, reacquainting myself with the place, but I avoid the wing with the ballroom. I'm not ready for that just yet. Despite everything that's happened to me over the last five years, it almost feels like I never left. Even with its stark, clean setting, it still feels cozy and more like home than my own.

"I can't believe she's actually here, the audacity of it all to show her face here."

"Yasmina, stop it! You don't know anything. You have no idea why she's here, and you are the last person who should judge. We all do things for our lands that we may not want to do, and not every piece of gossip you hear is truth either." I hear Centra's voice ring out as she scolds her older sister.

"I know what I heard, and what I heard is that she was caught with that *beast*. What sort of self-respecting person does that? And even if she wasn't, her being here is still weird. Everyone knows the history between the Vasaras and the Daarkes. It's not exactly a secret."

"Did you ever think that maybe it's just as hard for her to be here as it is for us? We've all had to leave something behind." I hear Talia speak up on my behalf as I continue to hide in the shadows.

"Hard for us? Hardly. One of us could be the next queen, and have you looked at Cade recently? Yeah, that's not exactly a hardship," Yasmina counters.

"Maybe some of us had other plans, other roads to take. Other loves to have." Arabella sighs wistfully.

"God, could you be any more dramatic. And if you don't want to be here, feel free to leave," Yasmina spits, and I already know I'm never going to like the Spring Princess.

"You might be here by choice, Yasmina. But some of us have other people counting on us and our actions," I say as I step around the corner into the atrium, the shock on her face is enough to satisfy me.

"And who's counting on you? Your dead brother? You already failed him. There's nobody left for you unless you're counting your filthy animal lover," Yasmina throws back at me, stealing my breath.

"Enough!" I turn and see Rohan behind me, his anger bleeds into the room. "I think, Yasmina, it is time for you to leave. I will notify my mother and brother that you will not be continuing with your stay here. Now get your things and get out of my sight." His voice booms, commanding the room, and Yasmina jumps and scurries away. Centra follows after her, silently leaving just the four of us.

"I'm sorry, Emilia." He steps forward and places a hand on my arm.

"You have nothing to apologize for, Rohan. They were not your words, plus, it's not like I've not heard worse."

"Still. I'm going to go and make sure she has all of her things and that she is leaving. I'll catch up with you later." He turns and strides from the room, and I take a seat opposite the two girls. Arabella sighs at Rohan's departure, and I get the feeling Cade isn't the prince that she'd pick if she had the choice.

"We're sorry too," Arabella says softly.

"Why?" I ask

"We didn't exactly jump to your defense," Talia tells me.

"Talia, I don't expect you to. You're here for your reasons, just like I'm here for mine. I'm under no illusions that we are all going to be best friends before this is over, that's not how this goes."

"Have you met with Lanora yet?" she asks me curiously.

"Not yet, have you?"

"Yes, I saw her straight after breakfast. It's just you left," she says, and I see one of the guards coming from the other end of the hall.

"I have a feeling my time is coming sooner than I had hoped." They look in the same direction and nod, before leaving me alone to my fate.

"Emilia?" he asks politely, but really, he already knows who I am. I stand and follow him towards Lanora's day room. Butterflies flutter in my stomach, and I try to smother them. Keeping my anger tempered down, my nerves in check, and a smile painted on might not be the hardest thing in the world to do in front of Rohan, but Lanora always saw everything you didn't want her to. Even the things you didn't know yourself. I don't think she ever used her powers on her sons, but I have no doubt she'll try to use them on me today, so this is going to be the hardest part of my lie. Remaining strong mentally, even if she taunts me with the things that are most likely to make me crumble. If I can't convince her that I want to be here, then I'm going home, and god only knows what else my father will think of to do to me once he has killed Oberon. Even if the treaty goes ahead, and Erion comes home safe and sound, I get the feeling he still won't let me be.

While I've been lost in my own thoughts, I've not been paying attention to my surroundings and nearly walk into the back of the guard in front of me. He opens the double doors to the day room, and ushers me inside before closing them behind me.

Soft music fills the room, joined with the singing of birds filtering in from the open doors to the gardens at the back of the rooms. I feel a pull towards the garden and can't stop my feet from moving. I've never been in here before, even in all the times I was here as a child. The lightness of the room surprises me considering its owner, but it makes me feel safer and lighter than I have in a long time. Like nothing outside of this room really matters.

"There you are, Emilia." I turn and see Queen Lanora descending the stairs from the mezzanine level of the room by the entryway, I hadn't even noticed it in my wonder of the gardens. She looks the same as she did, except harder. The lines of her face seem sharper with her blonde hair pulled back, and her eyes more scathing. "I have to admit, I didn't think you'd come."

"We all have our roles to play," I tell her honestly.

"That much is very true, but I have to wonder exactly what role it is you're here to play. You're not like the others. We have history, your family and mine. You and Cade were once close. That makes me question your presence here even more than the other sniveling little brats."

"I will tell you what I told Rohan, I am here *because* of our history. The people of Rivinea have been through so much over what seems like a millennium, and that sort of distrust and dislike will be hard to overcome. If our people can see that my family and yours can put the past behind us, forgive and move forward, everything considered, then there is no reason that they can't do the same. Our history isn't exactly a secret, so the joining of our houses would be even more significant than just the joining of two courts."

"And I'm sure Erion coming home would please your parents?"

"Of course, it would. My family lost a lot over those few days," I tell her honestly.

"And they don't mind sacrificing their only daughter?"

"I don't think they see it as a sacrifice. It is all for the greater good."

"I have heard rumors of the changes in your parents since that day. Stories of their parties reach even the furthest of ears," she pries, and I try not to flinch.

"Rumors are nothing more than that. My parents are fine. Of course, they grieve for one of their sons, and have hope for the safe return of the other." She circles me, assessing my responses, and I try not to hold my breath. I feel her presence on the outskirts of my mind as she tries to pry, to get inside and find out what she truly wants to know, but thanks to my grandmother's teachings as a child, my walls are basically impenetrable.

"Tell me, Emilia. Is it hard for you being back here? Knowing that if you're successful in this game of my husband's, you'll live in the place where your twin brother was killed?" Her question is followed by another mental assault, and I focus on keeping her out while grinding out my answer.

"Of course, it is, but I knew it would be. Remaining bitter and full of hatred about things I have no control of and can't change isn't going to get me, or our courts anywhere. I hold no ill will towards you or your family. I want to stop the wars, stop the suffering of our lands. You said yourself, Cade and I were close once, I don't see any reason we can't be again. I've already been reconnecting with Rohan, so I see no problem with moving past our history." The lies taste like copper on my tongue, but I keep my pain nestled down inside me, where it will need to stay, forever possibly.

"You're not like the other girls, they were all so easy to read."

"I imagine they were, they're not as familiar with your... talents as I am."

"Yes, well, there are still many things that you do not

know, Emilia. Remember that during your time here. You can leave now." She waves a hand, and the main doors to the room open again as I am dismissed. Relief pours through me, and I head towards the exit and my respite.

"Oh, and I heard Rohan already dismissed one of the girls because of you, Emilia," her voice rings out behind me. "Be careful to remember which of my sons you're meant to be here for."

6

I've been here for a week, and I already want to claw my eyes out and risk my father's wrath. All it has consisted of is time alone, or with the other potentials for Cade's wife. I have not seen even a whisper of Rohan or Cade, or much of anyone except for Cibyl, who is apparently our keeper and is in charge of making sure we stay in line. She's also the one who informed us yesterday there will be a public presentation this week to the Royal families from both courts, where we get to present ourselves officially to Cade and essentially parade around and show why he should pick us. Rumors have been flying around here about the health of the king, and I can't help but wonder if that's why we've not seen any of the Vasaras. I try not to take much stock of rumors, but when I have nothing else to busy my mind, it's hard not to speculate and distract myself from the ridiculous notion of presenting myself.

It's fucking archaic and belittling, and I have no choice but to be on my best behavior. My father will be there, watching, making sure I'm keeping up my end of our deal, though I have no idea if he is keeping his. For all I know, Oberon is already dead, what's worse is I wouldn't put it past my father, but I have to hope that he's keeping his word.

I stare up at the ceiling, I know I should get dressed, prepare for the day, but I honestly have no will to move. The door bursts open, and I gather the duvet under my chin.

"Wakey, wakey, Emilia. Ladies do not laze in bed all day, we have much to do before your presentation this evening!" Cibyl bursts into my room like the unwanted ray of sunshine that she is, and flings the curtains back, my eyes water at the sudden brightness.

"It's not even that late, Cibyl." I sigh, resigned to the fact that my hope of doing nothing is shattered, and pull back the duvet. "And what do you mean the presentation is tonight?"

"It's really not that hard to understand." She tuts at me and continues muttering to herself, as she dives into my closet before emerging with what I'm assuming are my choices for this god-awful day.

"I'm a big girl, Cibyl. I can pick my own clothes." I stand and stretch as she eyes me with disapproval.

"Yes, well so far today all you've done is stay in bed, and it's already midday! Your behavior doesn't exactly scream queenly, princess or not. Now will you please get yourself cleaned up, we have to go meet Master Rohan before we start the preparations for tonight, and everyone is waiting on you!" She thrusts a black dress into my hands and shoos me into the bathroom, where I lock the door to keep her out. I lean back against the door and take a deep breath. This is going to be a long day.

We walk through the familiar maze that is the Winter Palace, and my pulse races as I realize where we're heading. I'm not ready. I thought I'd have more time before I saw it, before I was back there. Panic claws up my throat, and I struggle to draw in breath. I try to fight the panic threatening to take hold of me as the edges of my eyesight darken, and I know I don't have long to get a hold of myself before I make a scene, and I hate the attention. I focus on three things. Three things I can see. Cibyl. The floor. My shoes. Three things I can feel. The smooth silkiness of my dress. The old, scratchy tapestry on the wall beside me. The smooth wall behind it. I take a deep breath, and I can feel myself starting to settle.

"Emilia, please. Come on, we're going to be late!" Cibyl scolds, with a disapproving tut. Obviously, she's not my number one fan and has no patience for my gentle sensibilities. It's one of the reasons I never really had any friends outside of my brothers and the Vasaras. Most Fae are hard, brutal, there are some like me, but most live in the realm of humans, where we can glamor ourselves and blend in. But for me, that was never really an option. I tried it for a while with my grandmother, but I grew too weak away from our world. No one really knows why, it's unheard of for our kind, but again, it was just another thing to make me even more of a weirdo in our community.

I hear Cibyl sigh, and start walking again to catch up with her, shoving down the dread I can feel bubbling away in my stomach again.

"Ah, Master Rohan, thank goodness we found you. Maybe your presence will incite the princess to get to where we need to be going."

"Cibyl, are you aware Emilia's brother was killed just steps from where we are? Have you considered that could be a reason for her lack of want to follow you hastily?" She pales at his words, not because of me, but I think for fear of being scalded by Rohan. "I think, that maybe you should apologize to Emilia, and maybe be more mindful during her stay here. After all, she could be your next queen."

I cover my mouth and cough to hide my snort of laughter that threatens to break the sinister outlay of Rohan's words. But then it hits me. I really could be the next queen. Holy shit.

"I apologize, Master Rohan. I did not know. I did not think."

"It is okay, Cibyl." I reach forward and touch her arm, and she jerks away from me. Sometimes I forget how warm my touch must feel to the Winter Fae.

"I'll take her from here, you'll just need to collect them before the presentation this evening," Rohan tells her before offering me his arm. "Are you okay?"

"I'll be fine, I just wasn't ready, and I had no time to prepare because I had no idea where we were going. Why does she hate me so much?" I look over my shoulder and see her figure disappear around a corner.

"Cade was always her favorite when we were growing up, and after everything happened, she saw what happened to Cade. I guess in some way, she holds you responsible for that, or at least your family."

"What do you mean, what happened to Cade?"

"Not my story to tell, sweetheart. Now let's get you to the others so we can get ready for this monstrosity later." I sigh and follow his lead, but if he thinks I'm going to forget, he's sorely mistaken.

I can't help but take a deep breath as we enter the ballroom. Now this room looks different, it looks so light. The walls are washed in white, with gold accents matching the exterior of the palace. I don't get a chance to get lost in my memories because the sound of the other girls hits me. There might only be three of them now, but my god can they cause a racket.

"Ladies." Rohan clears his throat, and they all go quiet. He releases my arm, and I go to stand with them, reminding me of my place in all of this. I'm just another pawn.

"Tonight, is going to be different from anything you have experienced, and there is going to be a lot of people here, I suggest you leave your humility in your rooms. My brother can be cruel, my father more so, and they're going to want to see just how far you are willing to go to be Queen of the Winter Court. It is no real secret that my father will be stepping down in a few years, so he and my mother want to make sure whoever takes their place has the stomach to do what is necessary for the realm, but they will also want you to be strong, regal, and most importantly, know yourself and what you are capable of." He lets it sink in before he continues, "This is not going to be easy, and I would urge you to consider all of these things before you walk through those doors this evening."

"But we're still Royalty, surely this won't be too bad? Our parents would never accept anything too insane," Arabella says, looking really quite terrified at the prospect of what could happen, and the reality of what she's signed herself up for.

"My father believes in the old ways. It doesn't matter who you are at Summer Court. Here, you are just a girl wanting to be queen. Your status whilst catered to here, is not really acknowledged in full. It is by grace that you are treated like Royalty while you are in our lands, but not by right or law."

"This is absurd. How bad will it really get? It's a presentation. I think you're just trying to scare us," Centra blurts out, her usually tan skin looking awfully pale.

"No, I am trying to prepare you. Now, if you wait two moments, your meals will be served to you in here, as there will not be time for food this evening. You will each be called from your rooms in turn, and if you are lucky enough to pass this evening, you will return to your room. If not, you will be escorted to collect your things and will be taken back home. Remember, this is what you signed up for. You are not forced to be here. You asked for this, and you can leave at any time."

As he finishes, the doors burst open and a ton of wait staff scurry into the room, preparing a table, and laying plates, before food is brought in.

"Enjoy yourselves, ladies. I will see you tonight," Rohan announces before his departure, sending me a sly wink before he turns and exits, leaving me with three now rather scared princesses. *Thanks, Rohan.*

I stand and stare at myself in the mirror before me, and wonder for the umpteenth time what the hell I'm doing here. Maybe I could confide in Rohan, and he would help me, but he could still also betray me. I have to remember that these people are not the friends I used to have. They betrayed me once, they can do it again. Being friends with them is something I have to pretend to do, and I can't get wrapped up in the lie of it all. I can never forget.

Sitting and waiting to face my undoubted humiliation tonight, I just need to keep a handle on my temper. I have a feeling burning the Royal family alive probably wouldn't go in my favor, though it could solve some problems I have. I laugh to myself at the absurdity of it all. Of all of this. At the fact that I'm still here, trusting my father to keep his word. I don't know if I'm being more than a little stupid, but all I have is hope that he's keeping his word. It's not like I can even ask anyone, the only person I have on my side outside of these four walls that isn't locked up is Lily, and she won't go near the cages no matter how much she loves me.

A knock on my door announces the arrival of my escort, and I pick up the blood-red shawl that matches my dress for the evening and open the door. A man dressed in full warrior armor stands waiting for me on the other side. He motions for me to walk and falls in line behind me when I do. These last few weeks have been so very bizarre, but this might just be the strangest thing yet. I've never seen the military guards at the palace, in either court. They are usually stationed on the front lines or at the cages. The pit of my stomach drops as unease washes over me, I can't put my finger on it, but something doesn't feel right, where are the Hunters? This is usually their job, not our soldiers. Surely Rohan would have told us if the guard were going to be here during his terrible pep talk this morning? I open my mouth to ask him, but I can't find the words. It is not my place here yet to ask such questions, but still, my head hurts with the questions swarming. I take a deep breath. *Concentrate Emilia! You have more important things to worry about right now.*

I round the corner and come face to face with two more guards on either side of the doors to the ballroom. I look to the mirror on my left and steady the gold leaf tiara woven into my hair, trying to calm the butterflies creating havoc inside me. The doors open, taking away my last seconds to compose myself, and then I'm drowned in light that follows me down the stairs as I descend into my personal hell. There are so many people in here. Royals and social climbers of the Winter Court, I try to see into the edge of the room, cast in shadows, but the light surrounding me blinds me from it. The applause continues as I make my way onto the stage, in front of the table where the Vasaras sit, with Cade to the left of his father, who is just an older, slightly graying version of Cade, and Rohan to the right by his mother. I curtsy as tradition dictates and hold my submissive position until I am released by King Earon's words.

"Emilia Daarke. What a long time it has been! Maybe this time, when you leave here, it will not be in bloody circumstances." His cruel smile takes up half of his face and I hear the laughter and spattering of applause from his audience behind me. I look to Lanora, whose face is unreadable. Cade sits stoically as if his father has said nothing, but I see Rohan wince slightly from the corner of my eye. I will not be baited, because that is exactly what they want.

"King Earon, it has been a long time. I'm glad the years have been kinder to me than it seems they've been to you," I say sweetly, my insult obvious, but I know these people, I grew up with them. Trading insults is nothing more than a game to them. He pauses, and a hush descends across the room before his laughter belts out, the sound bouncing across the room, and I breathe a little easier knowing I've started well, and I'm not bleeding yet. Insulting the Winter Fae is a dangerous game. Sometimes they laugh, other times, they'll kill you where you stand. Blood sport is nothing unusual to them.

Cade stands and circles me, blatantly taking in my form in the corseted dress, which hugs and accentuates every curve I have, trying to demean me without words. I stand and take it, being treated like a piece of meat, as is expected.

"You, Emilia, chose to return here after your twin brother was slaughtered here at my own hand, and yet, you still wish to marry me and become the queen of this court. Is that right?" Cade faces the audience rather than me, everything for their entertainment, and to make me feel like less than nothing.

"That is right, but must you really treat me with such

disrespect. Someone who could potentially be your future wife, your future queen. Can you not even look at me when you address me?" I don't see his hand as it reaches out and strikes me across the face, lightning fast, the shock of it knocking me off balance.

"Maybe you are the one who needs to learn some respect, to the future king of this court, and to the man you are hoping to marry. Know your place." He towers over me, and that's when I work out his game. He wants us to submit, to show that we are weak and unworthy of him. So, I brace myself and stand.

"My place, your highness," I spit, "is not on my knees, or at your feet." I stand tall and take him face on. "No queen of your court or mine is a submissive coward. I was not raised to cower before you, but to be the strength and power at your side."

His father claps, and the audience roars with cheers and applause. This farce is insane, but I swallow down my disgust at the ridiculousness of it all and smile sweetly as Cade takes his seat by his father again. I wait quietly for the room to quiet, when Queen Lanora smiles at me, but her smile gives me shivers.

"Are you a virgin, Emilia?"

"I'm not sure why that is of concern here." I hide my clenched fists in the fold of fabric in the skirt of my dress and try not to show my anger at such a personal question in such a public forum. I know Rohan told us they would try to humiliate us, but this is just unnecessary.

"It is of concern because I asked you the question."

"And would you respect your future queen if I actually answered your questions in a forum like this? I know I wouldn't. So, you can ask your questions, but I do not have to answer them."

"Touché. But still, you have not answered my question. Maybe you'll answer this one, what would you sacrifice for your place here as queen?"

"More than you know," I tell her with a heavy heart, knowing I'm already sacrificing my love for Oberon, my chances of a life far from here.

"Would you sacrifice the life of your last living brother?" She waves her hand and two of the guards disappear, reappearing with Erion, bloody and beaten, in those god-fucking-awful magikal binding cuffs.

"Erion," I gasp and take a step forward, but I am pulled backwards by Cade and locked in his grasp. I can do nothing as my brother is thrown to the floor at my feet, and Lanora stands over him. I watch in horror as she takes a handful of his knotted, dirty hair and yanks his head backwards exposing his throat. She places her metal-clad finger at his throat, the sharp point of the tip glinting in the light. I can almost feel the bloodlust from the people in the room, hoping beyond hope that Lanora will slice through his flesh, and drain him.

"You must decide, is his life worth more to you than your position here?" she taunts me, and I struggle in Cade's grip, but he tightens it. I look down at Erion, who doesn't really look like my brother anymore. The man I remember stood tall like a giant, he was strong and passionate. A protector. But this man, he seems small and weak. The fire that once burned in his green eyes is nothing but dull embers, and my heart breaks over what they might have done to him to have broken him as much as they have. Seeing my brother reduced to this makes the fire inside me burn stronger, I can feel the fire raging, desperate to be released to reign down my own version of justice and revenge for what they've done to him.

"Careful, Emilia," he whispers into my hair. "Stay true to yourself, all is not what it seems."

"I will not risk his life. He is the reason I am here. Him and so many other innocent lives fighting in our stupid war. I am here to stop the inane fighting and unnecessary bloodshed that continues because our courts cannot seem to grow up enough to find peace and stop sacrificing those who have nothing to do with the disagreements of our ancestors. Why should my brother, or any of the many others we have down at the borders, lose their lives for such an unnecessary and archaic argument that none of us were even present for? Hell, I don't even know why this craziness originally started, the insane hatred between our courts, but if I have the power to end it, I will. But not with more bloodshed. I will not be responsible for that."

Lanora's eyes dance in the light as she releases my brother, who looks up at me like he's already dead. All these years, we thought he was at the front, so how is he here? How long has he been here? Did my father know he was here? So many questions swirl through my mind as Cade releases me, and I fall down to my brother and wrap him in my arms.

"I am so sorry, Erion," I tell him as I hold him tightly. He doesn't return my embrace, he just kneels lifelessly. "I'll bring you back, just you wait and see."

"Please just let me die," he murmurs as I let him go, and my heart breaks all over again, my rage simmers just under the surface at what these people have done to my family.

"Release him," I demand from my crouched position by my brother in front of Lanora.

"We will do no such thing at this time."

"Mother," Rohan interjects but is silenced with a look from Lanora. I hear the murmurings around the room, but I don't care.

"Please, look at him! He cannot take much more of whatever has happened to him. At least let me take him back to my rooms and care for him," I beg, my voice little more than a whisper, desperation winning over my rage.

"I said no. You are a guest here, you should remember that." She signals, and the two guards who brought Erion here lift him, one on each arm, and start to drag him away. Cade releases me and sits back down with his family, his face unreadable.

"This is not right. He is a Prince of the Summer

court." My fire burns bright as my hands feel the lick of the flames that surround them. I look over at the Vasaras as Earon whispers to Cade, who doesn't look happy, but he nods, nonetheless.

"A queen should be able to control her temper, Emilia. Apparently, you cannot. Look at you, anger is an undignified response and nothing like the girl I once knew. Your time here is over," Cade announces, and shame fills me, distinguishing my flames. What have I done? Have I just sacrificed the lives of my brother, and Oberon, just because I couldn't get my way?

"No, please. I'm sorry, I didn't mean…"

"Enough, Emilia. Leave here now." I look frantically over to a forlorn Rohan, whose face shows me just how much I fucked up, and I try not to act like a spoiled child as the guard comes to escort me away. There has to be a way I can fix this. There just has to be.

I pace in my room, waiting for someone to arrive, to escort me home. It feels like hours since they took Erion away, and Cade cast me out. I wonder if my father has heard, and what his reaction will be if he has. I pull at my dress, not caring about damaging it. I just need out of its confines. I need to breathe. I need to be able to think. Maybe if I speak to Cade, he'll change his mind. Who am I kidding, he's never going to change his mind? I tear the material binding me and frantically rip the dress off, grabbing a gown and draping it over my shoulders, so I'm not half-naked when whoever is coming appears.

I'm very aware I need to compose myself, but I feel like I'm spiraling, so I sit on the stool at the dressing table and pull the pins out of my hair. I take the golden leaf crown from my head, placing it down as gently as I can before I wipe this crap from my face. I've never really been a fan of makeup, but it gives me the mask I so desperately needed here, though even that didn't help.

I stand as a knock on the door sounds, and it opens. Rohan appears before me, looking more than a little flustered, slamming the door behind him.

"Emilia, fuck!" He pushes his hand through his hair, and I can feel just how off-kilter he is. "What a fucking nightmare. I didn't know about Erion, I'm so sorry. If I'd have known, I would have told you."

"It's okay, Rohan. I believe you." And I did. Rohan doesn't seem to be much like his father and brother. He's more like me than I've ever realized, being the odd one out. I place my hand on his shoulder, and he pulls me into a hug. I can almost feel his power humming under his skin, and his desperation gives me something else to focus on.

"It's going to be okay," I tell him. I'm lying, and he knows it, but I think he also needs to hear it.

"They're going to send you home in the morning, it's too late to pull out the horses, but that might give us some time to salvage this. Those other girls, honestly, Em... None of them are fit to be queen. If you'd have seen the things they did, the way they debased themselves for him. It turns my stomach. Who does that to their future wife? I swear I don't even know my brother anymore. I know this was mainly my father, pulling his strings as ever, but to do what they did to those girls. I don't even want to be near them, but I also know that someone needs to stay here and keep Cade true. Remind him who he really is underneath it all, outside of my father's whispers and lies. You can't leave Emilia, you're the only one who reminds him of who he used to be. The man he wanted to be. The king he wanted to be." He paces in front of me, and I let him rant.

"You have to remember who he once was. Yes, he was an ass, but underneath it all, he was good. He hated the games my father played, the cruelty of it all. Once upon a time, he wanted to change things for the better. He wanted to join the courts, to bring peace to the realm once and for all. But my father has twisted him, used the guilt from Edimere to create a monster. Cade doesn't think there's any good left in him, he doesn't see how lost he is. When I saw your name on that stupid list, I foolishly had hope. I should've known they'd come up with any reason to cast you out. My father was never going to let you stay. You'd have either been too strong-willed, too submissive, too disruptive. God I'm such an idiot, I should've seen it coming, I never should've brought you here. I'm so sorry, Emilia. I will get Erion out of here alive and back to your family. Don't ask me how, but I will do it. This craziness has to stop."

"Can you get Cade to change his mind? Or at least agree to see me?" I ask him once he stills.

"I can get him to see you, but you'll have to change his mind, Emilia. They already know I'm biased when it comes to you. They think my guilt fuels me to champion for you, but they can't see the truth." He looks at me, and I have to look away, unable to face what he's telling me without saying a word. I don't have room for complications, and that's what this is.

"I forgive you, Rohan. I already told you that, but I'm here for Cade, for my brother, and for the realm." I take a deep breath, preparing to trust one of the people I swore I would never trust again, but I find that my words aren't a lie, and I have forgiven him. Rohan was just a child, and I think Lily was right, it was his father who was responsible for the situation he was placed in. Being back here and seeing Erion the way he was tonight has given me a sort of clarity about the real monsters here.

A knock interrupts us, and Rohan opens the door.

"A package for Miss Emilia, sir," a deep voice says, I don't see whoever is there, blocked by Rohan who takes the package and closes the door once again. He strides across the room and gives it to me, where I sit on the bed. I look at the note attached.

Remember what is at stake, Emilia. Here's a little reminder to encourage you to fix your mess.

. . .

I undo the ribbon on the gold box and lift the lid, before screaming and dropping the box. My stomach turns as I try to stop the bile rising up. Rohan reaches down and opens the box showing me the piece of bloody, torn flesh with the tattooed mark of the Hunter. His face flits with confusion as he reads the note before he looks at me again.

"Emilia, what the hell is going on?"

"Rohan, I can't…" I might have forgiven him, but can I trust him with this? Will he still look at me the same?

"Emilia, I might be the only person inside this fucking place on your side, so be honest with me right the fuck now." He puts the lid back on the box and places it on the dressing table across the room, so I can't see it. I can still feel myself shaking. *Oberon, what have they done to you? I am so sorry.*

I can feel the tremor in my hands, the fear for Oberon, the anger at my father for his rash actions, and hopelessness at my position right now.

"Rohan… If I tell you, you can't tell anyone. I need you to promise me," I utter, preparing myself to trust one of the people I swore I would never trust again.

Rohan stares at me, trying to take in everything I just told him. How my parents changed after Edimere. What life has been like, and what they made me do to that poor girl at that stupid party. Oberon. The reasons I really came here. Once I started, I couldn't seem to stop, and now there's nothing left for me to say, but he's just sitting there staring at me like I have two heads.

"You fell in love with a… Hunter?" His words are slow, and I can almost feel the confusion.

"Hunters are people too, you know. And just like us, they're not all the same. Not at all what people think they are," I half-scold him, but it's not his fault. We're all taught that Hunters are beneath us, nothing more than dogs at our beck and call.

"Hey, I didn't mean it that way. I just never would've pictured it, that's all. Plus, everything you just hit me with… that you were just going to leave everything behind. It's a lot to take in, Em."

"I know, but god, if you'd seen the people my parents had really become."

"I got a good look that night I picked you up. I didn't know why you'd gone all flamethrower on the party, but now I do, and it all makes a lot more sense. I'm sorry everything got so bad for you."

"It's not your fault, Rohan. They're grown-ass people, they knew what they were doing, grief only excuses them so far. It showed me where Edi got it from, ya know, I always wondered because back then, my parents weren't like they are now, but I guess the darkness was inside of them all along. Though my main problem right now is convincing Cade not to give up on me."

"You're not wrong. It's probably not going to be easy, but this is you and Cade. You guys were always pulled together, he was drawn to you like a moth to your flame, no matter how much he fought it. I also don't think he knew about Erion. Those two used to be closer than he and I have ever been, I imagine it killed him seeing Erion like that."

"I don't know about all of that, especially if he's changed as much as you've said, but maybe the Cade I used to know is still in there somewhere. I just need to reach him."

"Come on, let's get you in something that's not going to expose you to half the palace, and sneak you to Cade. Though... the robe might be a good plan." He smiles, trying to lighten the moment, and I playfully slap his arm.

"Some things really never do change, huh." I shake my head and walk to my closet, pulling on a pair of skinny black jeans and long gray shrug sweater, and pull on a pair of boots. I sweep my hair up into a ponytail before leaving the small room and come face to face with Rohan.

"Right, I'll do, I'm half way to presentable. Now let's go see your brother, I guess."

"Okay, just please be careful, Emilia. I told you, he isn't exactly who you remember. You've seen. I'll just hope you can reach him."

Rohan walks with me towards Cade's rooms but leaves me to face him on my own. I wring out my hands, trying to settle the nerves fighting to break through. I can do this, I *have* to do this. I raise a hand to knock on the dark wood door to his bedroom, but it opens before I make contact, and I come face to face with Lex, who greets me with a sneer.

"What do you want?"

"Obviously, I'm here to see, Cade, not you." There's just something about this guy that gets my back up. I've only seen him a handful of times but considering those few times, and what Rohan told me, he seems like poison. A perpetual bad mood hanging around Cade.

"He doesn't want to see you. He dismissed you, so I suggest you scurry back to your room and get packed up."

"Cade!" I shout, this dickwad needs to get out of my way, but I'm trying not to lose my temper. Lex steps forward and grabs me by the throat, lifting me from the floor to his eye level, about two feet from the floor. I struggle to breathe and claw at his hand, kicking out to try and make him release me, but all I can focus on is the pain, and that I can't breathe. He pulls me closer to his face.

"You listen to me, you piece of fucking Summer scum. You are nothing, and Cade is better off with you gone, so you're going to be gone. And if you don't, this is nothing. You've never known anyone like me, Princess, I don't care what you've seen, or what you've been through, it will be nothing compared to the hell I'll make your life if you cross me." He drops me to my feet and steps back as I grasp my throat and suck in oxygen. Cade appears in the doorway and takes in the scene, he looks confused but doesn't question it.

"Why are you here, Emilia?" He drags his hand down his face, and I see how tired he is. The sharpness of his words halts me until I remember that I'm not here just for me.

"I just wanted to talk to you before I have to leave."

"I don't have anything else to say to you, Emilia." He looks over me, his eyes barely taking me in, and glances at Lex before looking back to me, the harshness of his voice reflected on his face.

"Well then, maybe you can just listen. It's been a long time, Cade. Give me five minutes, for old times' sake?" I plead, and I can see the glee in Lex's eyes at my pleading.

"I said no, Emilia," he dismisses me then goes back into his room and slams the door behind him. I push down the urge to cry out in frustration, I will not show any kind of weakness in front of Lex. Instead, I straighten myself, wincing slightly at the pain of my throat, and consider my options. What the fuck am I going to do now?

I stay standing where I am and wait for Lex to leave, which he does after staring me out thoroughly, trying to scare me further without words. If only he knew the monsters I've fought, his kind of scary doesn't even come close. "You're wasting your time, but if you want to stand outside his rooms all day, go ahead."

I watch as his back disappears around the corner down the hall before softly knocking at Cade's door again. I wait, hoping he'll open it, but I can feel deep down that I'm clutching at straws. I lean against the door and slide down, my jeans and jumper giving me some needed warmth. I rest my head against the doorframe and wrap my arms around my knees as I settle in. He can't ignore me forever.

"For god's sake, Emilia!" I hear as I wake, falling backwards. I scramble to try and not hit the floor, trying to get up before I get tangled in my tired state and trip forward, plowing straight into Cade.

"I am so sorry!" I can feel the redness climb up my throat and warm my cheeks. I've never been the most graceful, but fuck my life, this is a whole different level for me. He holds my waist steady and firm as I right myself, I look up at him and my breath escapes me. I forgot how his eyes were flecked with gold, how deep they were, as if I was looking inside of him.

"What do you want, Emilia?" It's almost a growl, and it sobers me to the situation. I step back and smooth down my clothes, wrinkled from being in that position all night.

"I tried to speak to you last night, I wanted to ask you to reconsider my position. Please, Cade. You have no idea how much this matters to me." My voice isn't much more than a rasp, I look back up at him, but his eyes are fixed on my throat, and I can see the rage burning brighter. I touch my neck and wince at the contact. I'd forgotten about Lex in my fluster. I don't want to think about what I look like right now.

"Who did that?" His voice is commanding, demanding an answer, but I look at him flatly. He must know, but I guess there wasn't any bruising last night. He steps towards me and his hand snakes behind my neck, and his thumb brushes the bruising gently. For a minute it's as if we're thrown into the past, and his eyes close to half-mast, the fire burning there, and just for a second, I think he's going to kiss me. Until he steps back and withdraws his hand as if I burned him.

"That doesn't matter, what's done is done. It's nothing, I need you to focus on what I'm saying, Cade. Please."

"It matters," he mutters, pulling his hand down his face, and that's when I see him again. My Cade. The one I used to know. The way he is looking at me is exactly how he looked at me the day we became friends. When a group of Fae had been pushing me around, pulling my hair, trying to cut me or bruise me, just because they could. He saved me that day, and we were friends from then on.

"It's not nothing, Emilia. You are a guest here, and despite what you might think, your safety is important to us."

"You already know who it was Cade, I don't need to tell you. That's not why I'm here." I look him straight in the eye, and I can see the conflict inside him. Granting my wish means going against his father. I hold my breath while I watch him think it over.

"Fine. You get a second chance, but you need to know that there's more coming, Emilia. I will not grant you this again. I won't be able to change my father's mind again if you don't play the game."

"Thank you, Cade." I rush forward without thinking, and hug him tightly. He's stiff as a board, but loosens after a few seconds, and runs his hand down my hair, his other arm circling me.

"If he hurts you again, you need to tell me." I nod, but I know I won't. I'm starting to succeed, I came here for a reason, and I'm not going to let something or someone like Lex get in my way.

"I mean it, Emilia. If anyone hurts you, you need to tell me."

"And what if the one who hurts me the most is you?" The words fall from my mouth before I can stop them.

"Then I shall carry that shame and burden with me and add it to the weight I already hold. I know I hurt you before Emilia. More than either of us wants to really admit out loud. I ruined all of those possibilities of what could have been, but I can't take it back."

I take a step back, his words stealing the breath in my lungs. What does that even mean?

"Good luck, Emilia. I truly hope that you can see past the monster I know you see when you look at me, despite everything. I never wanted to be the thing that you ran

from, just the man you ran to that made your heart sing."
He steps forward, and I take another step back, into the
hall, and he closes the door softly, putting the barrier back
between us.

What the fuck was that?

8

*I*t's been a few days since Cade granted my wish and confused me more than I ever thought possible. It seems it's still the four of us battling it out. I'm more shocked that it hasn't got tenser. The three of them seem genuinely friendly to each other, as for me, well, I'm nice enough, but I don't want to get too close. I don't need any more complications than necessary. I climb out of the shower, wrapping the fluffy white towel around me and pad into the room. I catch sight of myself in the mirror, and I can't help but stare. The bruises around my neck have faded to a sickly yellow-green, luckily the weather has turned colder, so no one has questioned my scarves. Something else seems different about me too, and I think it's my eyes. I don't look as angry as I have in the last few years. I think being here has changed a part of me. I've had the chance to get to know these people again, and I've started to move past my grief. The knowledge shocks me, but at the same time, it feels right to be moving past it after all of this time. While I'd still rather be back on that beach with Oberon, being here now isn't the worst place in the world.

I lift my head at the sound of my door opening and see Rohan's head peek in, he sees me with a blush creeping up his cheeks, and he closes his eyes.

"Sorry, I didn't mean… I mean, hi. I came to tell you we're having a dinner tonight. The family and the four of you. I just wanted to let you know, because obviously my father is my father, and I wanted to give you a heads up before Cybil arrives in about an hour and surprises you with it." I pull my towel tighter and smile at him.

"Thank you. I guess I better get myself presentable."

"You look beautiful, Emilia. You always do," he murmurs, pulling the door closed and leaving me alone again. I sit on the bed, and Lanora's words haunt me, *"Remember which of my sons you're here for…"* I don't want to overcomplicate what is already a ridiculous mess, I don't want Rohan to get hurt, plus he's my only real ally here. I need to stop this before it gets any more complicated.

I stand with purpose, my first hurdle is tonight's dinner, I'll worry about everything else after. I exchange my towels for my robe and then sit and dry my hair, carefully pulling it backwards into rolls, weaving white baby's breath from the vase of flowers on the mantel into the back on my hair. I place my black tiara in the front of my hair and let curled strands fall down and frame my face. I paint my face with dark eyes and light lips, highlighting the strong lines of my cheekbones but softening my jaw. I study my reflection, and I look almost identical to how I did the night Edimere died, the only real difference is my eyes. The blue looks darker, older, wiser now. I'm not a glassy-eyed girl crushing on a boy, hoping he might want her too.

A knock raps on my door, and I smile as Cybil enters looking flustered.

"Dinner, tonight. With the Vasaras in the main dining room. Be ready in twenty minutes." She eyes me up and down with a disapproving frown, working out that this isn't as last minute for me as it is for her, but I smile at her regardless.

"Yes, of course. I'll be ready to go in ten." I stand and close the door as she harrumphs in the hall, it's a tiny win, but I'll take it. That woman has been getting on my last nerve. I pad over to my closet and look through the many dresses in here that were picked for me and put in here. I don't know who picked them, but whoever did must've known me slightly. Each dress is one I would've picked for myself, all in dark, rich colors. I pull out the deep royal blue one that almost matches my eyes, and I know that's the one for tonight. I slide it off the hanger and step into the silky material, pulling it up and looping my arm through the thick straps. I struggle with the zip, but once it's up, I take a step back and look at myself in the mirror. I'm the eldest of all of the princesses here, not that the others are children, but they haven't lived life fully, and it shows. I take in my reflection, and I look ready to take on the world. To go to war. I open the door and stroll into the hall, my head held high. Tonight, I'll show them what I'm really made of. Tonight, I'll prove why I'm meant to be here. Tonight, I'll save Oberon and Erion's lives.

I glide towards the main dining hall unaccompanied, a feeling I relish as it's rare I don't have an escort these days. I reach the main doors and bow my head to the guards standing there, who nod back and open a door each in turn. I enter the room, and I see the Vasaras sitting around the top of the table, but I am the first guest to enter. I walk towards the table, keeping my head held high. King Earon sits at the head of the table, with Lanora to his right, and Cade to his left, while Rohan sits to Lanora's left. I curtsy when I reach the table, waiting for an instruction of where to sit, handing the power over my evening to them temporarily. Cade and Rohan both stand at my approach, but Earon waves at them to sit.

"Emilia, nice of you to join us," he says with a sneer. "Though I was sure you'd been dismissed previously. My mistake, I guess. Please, take a seat." The displeasure drips from his words as I take a seat next to Cade and opposite Rohan when the doors open again, and the other three girls arrive with an even further flustered Cybil. I smile at her sweetly and she glares once she sees me.

Arabella, Talia, and Centra make their way towards us and the princes stand again, until they sit. Centra sits next to me, with Talia opposite Earon at the foot of the table leaving Arabella to sit next to Rohan, and she blushes slightly as she sits.

"Thank you all for joining us this evening," Earon says to the three of them, raising his glass of clear fizz, which I just know is nectar to them. "A toast, to my sons. For becoming the men I wanted them to be, and to Cade, the next King of the Winter Palace." At his toast, the serving doors burst open, and a dozen people flit about the room, refilling glasses and placing down dishes before scurrying away as if staying too long will cause them a great deal of pain, and I guess it would if they stepped out of line here. King Earon's temper is legendary, and as I know firsthand, brutality is his favorite game. Add the nectar to his normal charming ways, and tonight has disaster written all over it. It's the most potent form of alcohol available in our realm, crafted with magik to give the drinker a true escape. To feel what humans feel when they drink alcohol in excess. I never understood the appeal, but apparently, King Earon has a taste for the stuff.

We wait for the king to start eating before lifting our cutlery. I don't feel particularly hungry, but not eating would be an offence to the hosts, so I swallow down enough of the soup in front of me to have made a dent in it. I avoid the conversations going on around me and keep my eyes down, I don't want to start anything tonight, I merely want to survive the dinner. This is meant to be war, and tonight is just another battle, and if I can avoid the king's brutality, then I'll take it as a win, even if that means sacrificing the others.

"Arabella, tell me," King Earon says, an evil glint in his eye. "What really brought you here? Was it the chance to marry my boy, Cade? Or was it so that you could get closer to his brother? Whore yourself out to both of them, in hopes that someone would love you. I can't say I'm surprised, your mother left you at such a young age, god only knows what it was like growing up with just your father. Did he teach you the ways of becoming a woman, I wonder? There were always rumors when he didn't take another lover after your mother. And after your performing skills at the presentation, I have to wonder where you learned to debase yourself in such a way."

"Father, stop," Cade growls. "Tonight is not about you and your games. It was meant to be a nice dinner, time to get to know each other."

"And what is it you think I'm doing if not getting to know our young Arabella?" He laughs, taking another glug of his nectar. Arabella bursts into tears and runs from the room.

"Well, another one bites the dust, I guess," he says as he finishes his glass and the servers reappear, taking away the soup dishes and placing platters of meats, lobster, and so many other things on the table in front of us. Cade sits back down next to me, and I can feel the anger radiating from him, and he communicates silently with Lanora, while Rohan looks like he'd just rather be anywhere but here.

"That, sir, was really quite unnecessary. Arabella might be the youngest and meekest of us all here, but what you did was beyond cruel. She could've been your future daughter-in-law. The mother of your grandchildren. And you disrespect her in such a way? It is not a surprise, so few wanted to step forward to marry your son. The fear he would become a disgrace to the crown as you are is a real one." Centra stands as she dresses down King Earon, trying to defend her friend. I almost miss the action as he picks up his steak knife and flicks his wrist, sending the knife flying towards her. It hits its target in the center of her chest as he stands and roars.

"Do not forget your place here, girl. You are nothing if we do not approve it. You do not get to speak to me like that, ever. Your lesson will be costly." He takes his seat again, before filling his plate with meat and fruit as Centra struggles to breathe beside me. I look frantically to the brothers and Lanora, who all stay seated.

"For fuck's sake," I mutter before grabbing Centra, making sure she doesn't dislodge the knife and take her to the guards at the door.

"Get the healers here quickly, otherwise, full-scale war is likely to descend on this court," I tell them as they take in the scene, and one of them runs off down the hall while the other takes Centra from me with a small grimace.

"Thank you," I tell him as I turn and walk back into the room to face the fallout of my actions.

I take my place next to Cade again quietly and catch his eye, he thanks me in the only way he can, but this is madness. Where is the headstrong Cade gone, and why the hell will no one stand up to Earon?

"Emilia, thank you for taking out the trash. You must join me for a glass." He raises his glass of nectar and clicks his fingers. A server appears and places a glass in front of me, I don't want to drink it, it's meant to be the most addictive substance to the Fae, but turning it down could jeopardize why I'm here. I smile, and it doesn't quite reach my eyes as I lift the glass to my lips and take a mouthful. The flavors burst inside my mouth, and I feel like I've not drank anything for a week, the dryness of my mouth urges me to drink more of the sweetness, but I put the glass down and grab my glass of water before I lose what's left of my self-restraint. Earon laughs as the nectar starts to affect me. I grip the table tightly as the edges of my sight start to blur. I try to remain calm, but I can feel my heart racing.

"What have you done?" Rohan demands opposite me, and while I'm glad he finally found his voice, I'd much rather he just get me out of here.

"Only got our princess here to loosen up a bit. Her parents certainly know how to party these days, you saw that for yourself, Rohan," I hear as Rohan curses, and I can almost feel the questioning gazes from Cade and

Lanora. "Maybe now she'll embrace her true nature and prove that she has what it takes to be one of us."

I open my eyes from my crouched position, the pounding in my head makes it hard to see. But not hard enough that I can't see it. The blood. It coats my hands and arms, the floor beneath me. I lift my head, my hair flinging behind me is matted, but now I see it all.

What have I done?

There are bodies scattered across the floor, some dismembered, some unrecognizable. I try to stand, but my legs fail me. This couldn't have been me. I wouldn't do this. That's when I feel him behind me, I spin around to face him, feeling as feral as I'm sure I look.

"What did you do?"

"Oh, I didn't do anything, Emilia. This was all you." There's a smug smile on his face, and I want to wipe it off. My rage flares, and it's like a whole new beast I've never felt before. I feel my fire come to the surface, and I know my eyes are glowing.

"You're lying. You did something. You must have, I wouldn't have done this."

"No, Emilia. This is the reality of being what you are. We all have a monster inside of us, yours just hasn't come out to play before. There's more to you than you know, than any of us know."

I feel a tear of anger and frustration run down my face, and I can almost taste my fear at his words. This can't be who I really am. Yes, my kind might be cruel by nature, but this is not who I am. I don't want to believe it, even as the memories from last night filter in. The nectar. King Earon's words about me being who I really am. No. I won't believe it. I stand and face him head-on, pulling on my anger to strengthen my shaking legs, to keep me strong.

"Then why don't I remember? How do I know any of this was really me? This could all be a ruse, a way to try and break me."

"That would be the nectar. You did exactly as my father predicted. Exactly what he wanted of you. You showed us the real you. The you that you hide inside, buried deep. Turns out you let her come out to play when you let go of your high standards and your graces. Thinking you were better than the rest of us." His cruel words cut me, but I can't believe I did this. I look at him closely, and his eyes give him away. He doesn't mean his words. I'm not sure when I started seeing him properly again, but I know in this moment that the connection Cade and I once had is still there.

"I did not do this, Cade. And you will not convince me otherwise." I cross my arms, the blood still coating my blue dress looks almost black, but I try not to think about it too much.

"I told you she wouldn't fall for your stupid test,

Mother," Rohan calls from behind me, and I see him and Lanora entering the room, barely even noticing the death and destruction before them. I wince as they kick aside the bodies, the blood soaking into the hem of Lanora's skirt.

"It needed to be done. I needed her to prove that she truly knew herself, and what she was capable of before I could allow her to be queen. A true queen knows her strengths, her weaknesses, and knows just how far she will go to protect her people, not just the ones she loves, but all of them. She will also question her king, when she knows the truth inside of her, it will keep him strong, and it will keep him true. Power is a dangerous weapon in the wrong hands."

"Can someone please tell me what the hell is going on, and why it is my head feels like someone stomped on it?" My exasperation is topped only by the fact that I'm trying to calm my rolling stomach from bringing up whatever is left in it as I feel the blood around my mouth drying. That's when everything goes dark. I blink to clear my vision, and I'm not in that room anymore, I'm in the library, on the cushions on the floor, Rohan's hand in one hand, Cade's in the other, Lanora opposite me. That's when it hit me. This was Rohan, his gift. I'd almost forgotten he could do it. Climbing inside someone's mind, making them believe what he shows you is real. It feels real, you can touch, taste, and breathe as if it's real, but the horrors he can project are worse than I ever want to think of. Still, he can also make the most painful of things seem like they're not real and take you to a happy place where the rest of the world doesn't exist—it's a powerful gift, and one he used to hate. It's not his entire arsenal, but I guess Lanora has been making him hone it.

"I'm sorry, Emilia." He looks sheepish, but I could tell he didn't really want to do this either.

"There's nothing to be sorry for, Rohan. She passed the test, she knew what she was in for when she signed up to become queen. Now the decision is your brother's." Lanora stood with her words and left the room, leaving me with the two of them.

"Who else passed the test?" I looked between them, both of them quiet.

"Talia," Cade tells me as he stands, holding a handout to me. I take it and pull myself to standing, my muscles aching.

"Well then, I guess you have a decision to make." I try not to sound bitter or desperate, but I've done all I can do, and knowing it comes down to me, and perky, perfect little Talia makes me sick to my stomach. Cade turns and leaves without another word, leaving me alone with Rohan.

"It's going to work out, Emilia. You'll see. He'd be an idiot not to pick you, Talia won't stand up to him. She won't push him."

"Maybe that's exactly why he'll pick her." I sigh and open the curtains in here, letting in the rays of sun as they bounce off the glistening white snow outside.

"I don't think so, Emilia. We could just tell him the truth." He stands beside me and leans against the window frame.

"You know I can't do that. I need him to pick me because he picks me. My father would know, I don't know how, but he would, and I can't risk that. Telling you was dangerous enough, but I trust you, Rohan."

"And you don't trust him?"

"I'm trying. I keep seeing glimpses of him. The Cade I used to know, I can see him in there, but it's like the man I knew is chained down and locked up. I don't know how to reach him, and the Cade I need. This Cade is distant, mistrusting, and I don't blame him. He's his father's son. The man your father wanted him to be. But I can see him struggling, and sometimes it's like he's the man I remember. He's two people in one body fighting to work out who he is, against who your father wants him to be."

"I know, and I feel partially responsible. Cade took on the brunt of my father's wants and needs after that night. I was deemed too weak, and so he left me alone, but that meant that Cade got all of it. The pressures, the demands. The expectations."

"This isn't your fault, Rohan. It's your father's. I just wish we knew a way to win this game."

9

"You know, I never know what I'm going to get with you," Cade says as he pulls out a chair for me to sit before taking a seat opposite me.

"Pot, meet kettle," I say to him with a small smile.

"I guess I somewhat deserve that."

"Somewhat?" I admonish. "Somewhat? Cade you have more personalities than anyone I've ever met!"

"That might be true, but you're not exactly the simplest person in the world, either." He laughs a little, but I can tell he still feels uncomfortable.

"There's so much I want to tell you, so much we haven't had a chance to talk about, but first, we need to talk about last night. I guess you heard that Centra and Arabella were dismissed?" he says as he pours me a glass of ice water. "Arabella can't leave yet though, so you'll still see her around."

"Okay, is Centra okay after everything?"

"She is, thank you for doing what you did. I wanted to help, but…"

"But your father is a worse adversary than Centra's family?" I finish his sentence, and he at least finds it in him to look ashamed.

"Uncle Cade!" The door to the sunroom bursts open and in runs a little boy, probably no older than four, who runs into Cade's arms and looks at him like he hangs the moon.

"Hey buddy, what are you doing here?" he asks, and it's like he's transformed into a completely different man. His walls fall, and his eyes shine bright with love for the little boy.

"Uncle Rohan said you'd be in here and that you were busy, but I know you'd want to see me because you love me."

"Oh, is that right?" The little boy squeals as Cade tickles him and they fall on the floor, Cade taking the blow and laughing with the boy.

"Sorry, Cade. He's so quick," Rohan pants as he reaches the room and does a double take when he sees me watching them, and the tickle fest quits as Cade acknowledges his brother.

"Errr…"

"Who's the pretty lady, Uncle Cade?" The boy says,

jumping up and walking towards me. He looks so familiar, it's haunting, but his smile is so carefree. I lean forward and hold out my hand to him.

"My name is Emilia, and who are you, young man?"

"I'm not a young man, I'm four!" he tells me with enthusiasm. "My name is Erion, and I think you're going to be my newest bestest friend." I gasp, trying to keep my surprise from my face as the little boy takes my hand and shakes it enthusiastically.

"Well, that's a great idea, Erion. I know someone else with that name, and he's very special to me too."

"I'm named after my dad. My Uncle Cade told me so. My dad is a hero, he's Uncle Cade's bestest friend in the whole world, but he's fighting the bad guys, keeping us safe."

"Is that so?" I choke out. "He sounds like a special guy."

"He is. I live with my mummy in the village, but I get to come here whenever I want to."

"That's enough, buddy. I think Rohan should take you to go see the horses, what do you think?"

"Yes, I love the horses. Do you want to come, Emilia?" He looks up at me with such innocence, I swallow the pain and confusion and smile at him. "Not right now, Erion. I need to speak to your Uncle Cade, but maybe next time, okay?"

"Okay," he says with a shrug before hugging Cade and running into Rohan's waiting arms. "Let's go horseys!"

Rohan has the grace to look guilty as fuck before he escapes, leaving me alone again with Cade.

"Are you fucking kidding me! How could you keep this from me? From my parents? What the fuck!" I shout at Cade, who holds his hands up in defense.

"We tried to tell you, we reached out, but your parents weren't interested Emilia, they thought it was just another lie. We never heard from you after that day."

"They what?" I choke out. My parents knew. How is that possible? They sent me here to get Erion back, there's no way they'd have left his son here. Is there? I sit back down, the shock taking over.

Cade kneels before me and tucks my hair back behind my ear. "We thought you knew, we didn't realize until you'd been here a few days."

"But I saw Erion the other night. He was broken, Cade." He winces and pulls back, making me look at him.

"That wasn't really him, Emilia. It was a projection. My father's powers, remember? It's like Rohan's, but different. He projected the image of those guards, of Erion, to you, to us. The audience was a projection too. The only people really there were you and my family."

"But I felt him. I heard him..." I whisper. This is all too much to take in. "Where is he?"

"It was your test. Father knew he wouldn't break you like he did the others. So, he used what he knew would work. I am sorry, for what it's worth. I'm sorry for everything."

"Where is he?" I ask again, trying to take this all in.

"Last I heard, he was promoted to General. Away from the front lines, but still in the battle."

"Does he know?" I have to know.

"He doesn't know a thing. He slept with a girl from Summer Court who was sent to the front lines to cheer up the men down there. She was a dancer. I don't know too much, but I know that it's his son. The girl came to me when she was pregnant, she begged for my help, so I sent her to your parents. Two days later, she was back at our door. We tried reaching out after but got no response."

I sit back, reeling. I have a nephew, and my parents knew. My entire world tilts on its axis, and I question everything my parents ever said about anything.

"How can I believe anything you say?" I cry, and he sighs, scrubbing his hand down his face.

"I might not have given you many reasons to trust me, Emilia, but I'm still the person I've always been. The person you used to know. You say I have more personalities than you can keep up with, but did you ever consider that I'm just doing what I have to do, playing the role I have to play to get by. To survive."

His words silence me because no, I hadn't considered that. I just assumed and went with Rohan had told me, it all fit with what I saw.

"None of this makes any sense." I cradle my head in my hands, this is all too much, and I'm totally confused.

"Look, my father doesn't know about Erion, and I do

what I must to keep my father happy. There's not much to it other than that. I wanted us to talk, but this wasn't how I saw this going. We need to talk some more about the future, but I need to go and keep my father busy until Erion leaves. We're not finished here." He grips my shoulders and makes me look at him before he disappears. What the fuck just happened?

Since Cade's confession, things have been strange at the Palace. I've barely seen anyone other than Talia and Arabella, who has been staying at the palace despite being dismissed. We've spent almost every day together, with Cybil learning the way the Winter Court palace runs on a daily basis, learning the things we'd need to know if we married Cade.

"Don't you guys think it's weird no one has seen the Vasaras for like two weeks?" Arabella asks quietly as we sit to have breakfast in the small dining room where I first met them all. "I heard that King Earon was ill, and that's why they've not seen us since that night."

"I'm sure if he was ill, they'd have called in the healers," Talia says before taking another bite of her toast. All eyes turn to me, and I just shrug. If I had any idea what was going on, I'd maybe share, but I'm just as in the dark as they are. I finish my coffee and just let them continue to gossip, much like how it's been the last two weeks. I've been nice, sure, but I'm not here for that, and all of these delays just make me nervous. I've not had any more surprises from my father, but god only knows what he's been up to.

As if on cue, Lanora appears in the doorway, and the room goes silent.

"Emilia, I need to speak to you. Please." I stand and follow her out of the room. She remains quiet as I follow her. The light in her room enhances the tiredness on her face.

"Is everything okay, Lanora?" I ask, I'm shocked by my concern, but she was always like a second mother to me, and during my time here, I'm moving past my grief, and starting to see these people for who they are again, rather than holding my prejudices against them.

"There are so many things you don't know, things you never needed to know, but now you need to know. Please, sit." She waves to the white table and chairs by the windows, and I sit while she paces in front of me.

"First things first, I know you know of some of my gifts, Emilia. One you don't know, that no one other than Earon knows, not even my boys, is that I have the gift of foretelling." I gasp, foretellers are rare, and are almost always killed to prevent any courts having the upper hand. "I know, so you must know the trust and faith I'm placing in you by telling you this, but I fear you need to know. I have seen something so horrific even I cannot bear it. A darkness is coming, Emilia. I can't see all of the details, people's choices change the future, so I can only see the path we're on right now, but we can't stay on this path."

"Lanora." I stand and take hold of her arms, stilling her. "Maybe you should sit too, you're not making much sense."

"I can't see everything, but what I can see, is that you're going to say yes to Cade, and if you do, a darkness like we haven't seen in centuries is going to descend on our world. Chaos will ensue and there will be blood. So much blood."

"I don't understand Lanora, why wouldn't you just tell Cade?"

"He can't know, I tried that, but I've seen that I won't change his mind, and he has never put much stock in foretelling. You know that as much as anyone. It has to be you."

"Have you seen what happens if I say no to him?" I question, and her face crumples.

"No," she whispers.

"Then you can't know that that's what makes the difference, Lanora. I have my own reasons for saying yes if he asks me. You can't ask me to do this."

"I can free your brother, whether you marry Cade or not. I know that's why you're here."

"That's not everything, Lanora. Please, don't ask this of me."

"This darkness will eat them alive, Emilia. It will destroy everything we've built, eradicate our world. You need to do this. There is no one else." She starts to shake before she collapses, her eyes roll backwards as she seizes on the floor. I run to the door and call for help. A group of people run into the room and start to move around her. I step back against the wall, shaken and confused by everything that just happened. Was Lanora telling the truth? Or is she really just ill? Could she just not want me to marry her son? I have so many questions and no way of getting any real answers. I need my friend.

10

"So, this is what life at the Winter Palace is like? Not too shabby at all," Lily jokes as she takes in my room. The past few days have been a whirlwind of people in and out of the palace, it feels like something is going on, but nobody is telling us anything. So, I wrote to Lily and asked her to visit. I'm not sure whether or not it's permitted, but at this point, I don't care. I'm sick of not seeing people I know, people I can trust.

"It's not exactly how it seems. This was my room before." Her eyes widen as she realizes what I mean, and she pulls me into a hug. I let her, because more than anything, I need it. Ever since Lanora told me about her visions, I've been off-kilter.

"I can't believe they put you back in here!"

"It's not all bad, at first I think it was a test, but really it became a familiar place for me to seek refuge. To reflect. I'm used to it again now."

"So, are you going to tell me why you asked me to come?" She looks at me in suspicion. One thing about my best friend is that she never beats around the bush, she doesn't believe in it. It's a waste of time as far as she's concerned, but sometimes it takes me off guard. I sit on the bed cross-legged, and she follows suit, sitting opposite me.

"Something happened…" I stall, I don't even really know where to start. So I start from when I arrived, and I spill my heart out about everything that's happened since I got here, the tests, getting my friend back in Rohan, telling him about Oberon, the lovely gift from my father, about my nephew—all of it. When I finish, I look up at a shell-shocked Lily.

"I don't… how… why… I can't even." She takes my hands and squeezes them as she tries to find the words.

"I know, and that's not all." I sigh. "Lanora called for me, and she told me something. I don't know if I can believe her, it seems so crazy, but you should have seen her, Lily. She was losing her mind at the thought of what might happen."

"You're not really making much sense, Em."

"I know, I don't want to say anything because it could put people in danger, but at the same time, I just don't know what to do." I bury my face in my hands and try to calm myself down. I don't want to fall to pieces right now, so I take a deep breath. "I need you to swear to me, make the unbreakable promise that what I tell you, you won't speak about with anyone but me."

"Holy shit, Em. What the hell is going on?"

"I need you to swear."

"I swear. Cross my heart, wherever I go, across the world or back home. The words uttered between us will not cross my lips with another, or this fair tale shall end with slaughter."

"I'm sorry, but thank you." I take a deep breath and try to center myself. "Lanora is a foreteller."

"What the fuck? How? How is she alive? I thought they were all executed?"

"The only one who knew was Earon, and now us. That's how. I don't know how she cloaked herself, or how she escaped the purge all those decades ago, but that's not it. She had a vision that our world will be shrouded in darkness and blood if I say yes to Cade."

"And what happens if you say no?"

"Other than my father killing Oberon? She doesn't know, she hasn't seen that outcome. She said it was all based on people's choices, and obviously, I want to save Oberon. I want to stop the war between our courts, and I want my brother to come home. But until I make that choice, she can't see the other side of it, and I'm not sure I can make that choice."

"Holy fucking shit, Em. This is insanity."

"I know, and now everyone's disappeared. After she

spoke to me, she started convulsing, it was as if she were possessed. I've never seen anything like it. She was taken to the medical wing, but that's been shut down and restricted. I'm not even sure if you're meant to be here, but I needed someone to speak to. Someone who isn't here every day, that isn't Cade's biggest fan, and most importantly, someone I trust with my life."

"I don't even know what to say, what are you going to do?"

"I have absolutely no idea." I sigh and throw myself backwards into my pillows.

"There's also probably something you should know…" I lift my head and look up at her, really look at her, and I see how stressed she looks.

"I'm sorry, I've barely let you speak. What's going on with you?"

"It's not so much as what's going on with me, more just what's happening at home. I didn't want to tell you, because you already have so much to deal with by just being here, but I also don't think not telling you is going to do us any good either…" She pauses, and I see how tired she looks and the slight shake in her hands. Pulling away the happy-go-lucky facade, I see my best friend, and I can't remember a time I've ever seen her like this.

"The Hunters… They know your father has Oberon, and it's causing unrest. There have been Fae slaughtering Hunters publicly to try and keep the others in check, to show them what happens when they step out of line, but all it's done is cause a bigger divide. The Hunters back home have mostly stopped their guarding duties, there have been raids on some of the Royal homes, so far, no one has died, but who knows how long that's going to last for. Soldiers have been brought back from the front lines with the Winter Court to replace the Hunters, raids on the Hunters quarters have happened, and things are getting out of control. They have demanded your father release Oberon from the cages, and that a new treaty be drawn, to make things fairer for them. They're tired of being treated the way they have been, and I think hearing Oberon's screams from the cages was their battle cry. I don't know how long it will take for the dissent to reach here, but while the Hunters have the far side of the Summer/Winter border, I think that this might be what it takes to unite them."

"We have to do something... I could speak to Cade. Or maybe to Rohan, see if there's anything we can do."

"But won't speaking to Cade mean you have to tell him everything?"

"Probably, but what's the point in ending one war just to start another? I'll think of something. I've heard whispers of unrest, and Cade has been away a lot. I thought it was just his mother, but I doubt this sort of thing is outside of his scope. The Hunters have been strangely absent here too, but I've tried not to focus on it. There's only so much I can carry on my shoulders, you know?"

"I'm sorry, Em. I didn't want to bring it to you, but I don't know what else to do. King Levoya is doing nothing to settle the Autumn Court. He's too busy up in his palace preparing for the end of summer to notice what's happening with his people. As far as he's concerned, he's done his job to stop the war between the courts, and now he deserves a reprieve. I tried speaking to Araya, but you know how she is. Politics and war aren't her strong suits. I know I shouldn't speak that way of the potential future queen, but it's true."

"Take a breath, you don't need to worry about this anymore. It shouldn't have been your place to start with. I'll do something, but you can stay here for now if you'd feel safer?"

"Thank you, but I can't leave my parents and my little sister. I might not be able to do much, but if something happened to them while I was tucked up here, safe and sound, I'd never forgive myself."

"I can understand that. I'll get an escort to take you back home, but just try and keep a low profile, and stay safe. If you need anything, come and find me." I walk her to the front of the grounds, our feet crunching in the gravel stones where the carriages await us.

"I will do, you stay safe too, Em. I couldn't stand it if something happened to you. I love you." She hugs me tightly and holds on a little longer than normal.

"I love you too, Lily. I'm sure it will be fine, just

please, please, stay safe. You're basically all I have left. I can't lose you too."

"I'm not going anywhere." She winks at me as she climbs up into the carriage. "Not even the hounds of hell could drag me away." She laughs before she closes the door but hangs out of the window. "In all seriousness, if anything happens, run. I'll do the same, and I'll meet you in our old place, the cliff point between the courts, okay?"

"Okay." I nod, trying not to worry too much about what could happen if the Hunters rebel. I wave down two of the main guards on patrol, again military and not Hunters, and I try not to think about it too much.

"Swear it?" She smiles, it not quite reaching her eyes, the worry obvious on her face.

"I swear. I'll see you soon."

"Until then. See you soon." I wave as she disappears from sight, her escort close behind her, and I try to get rid of the foreboding feeling that I might not see her again.

11

I turn at the sound of a knock at my door and find Cade opening it slowly.

"Hey," he says softly.

"Hey, stranger." I walk to him and wrap my arms around him, feeling him relax a little at my touch. I'm trying my best to be the person I'm meant to be, but it's starting to be hard to differentiate between who I am and who I'm meant to be.

"Do you want to go for a walk? I know I've not had much time to spend with you recently," he asks as he steps back, putting distance between us again.

"Sure, let me just grab my shoes." I wander into the closet to find some flat boots, I'm not exactly dressed as a princess, but I also know that he's never really cared about that. At least he never used to. I pull the boots on over my jeans and grab a jacket before heading back out. He opens the door for me and waves me out of the room, ever the gentleman. It makes me wonder how much of this is Cade, and how much of this is the duty of the Winter Prince. He leads me through the palace and down through the staff quarters, which lead out to the grounds. I've always loved it back here, there are so many trees, it's like a sort of snowy forest paradise.

"How have you been finding things at the palace?" he asks as we walk towards the forest.

"Oh, I mean, it's okay. It's kind of what I expected it to be, but not at the same time, you know?"

"I think so. And you don't miss home?" He looks concerned, at least I think he does.

"The Summer Palace hasn't really been home in a while." I sigh. "I miss Lily, my friend from Avaenora, but there really isn't much for me back there, so no, I don't miss it."

"What about you? You've been super busy this last week?" I ask, trying to pry because one thing about being here is that I have almost no idea about what is going on in Eressea, and I hate it. He nods a little, looking out across the snowy lawns.

He barely reacts, and I can't blame him. This entire situation feels so awkward. I want to ask him questions, but I also don't want to pry, especially since he's barely said anything about where he's been, and absolutely nothing about what is going on, so I try to make light conversation.

"So, this is what being the Crowned Prince is like?" I force a laugh as we stroll across the grounds, and I try not to think about everything Lily told me earlier. "It's all having women fight over you and having your pick. Dinners, fancy parties, and picnics in the gardens. Doesn't sound so bad." I'm trying to keep things light. Today is my designated date day with Cade. Time for Talia and me to spend a day with him so he can get to know us better before our next and final test. I'm burning to ask him questions, more questions about what is really going on, to see if he knows already, but I know he won't share with me till he's ready.

"That's hardly all I do. That just happens to be this month, as we wind up towards the hard winter. It's my free time to get myself prepared for what is to come. These last few days are just unusual circumstances, but I do what I have to, to keep everyone happy and keep this place running smoothly."

"So, you don't ever really get downtime?" He doesn't answer, just keeps moving toward the blanket, held down by four heaters and a picnic basket I can see set up not far from us. I can't help but feel a little sad for him. So much changed for him too after the day he killed Edimere. He cemented his role in his family. The protector. His father's heir.

"Do you ever regret it?" The words slip out, and I see

his guards slamming back into place. "Sorry, forget I asked. That was stupid."

"No." I look at him, and this is the new Cade. The serious but heartless man he wears to protect himself. "I don't regret killing your brother." The words are like a knife to the heart, but I don't know why I expected anything else.

"Do I regret ever being put in that situation? Losing my best friend, and you all in one simple moment. That I regret. But I'll never regret saving Rohan's life. Saving him from having to fight for his life, potentially have to kill one of his closest friends. He was always the lightest of us all, with the biggest heart. It would have broken him to have to do that. So no, I don't regret it. I look at who he is today, and I know that sparing him that was the right thing to do. We have enough darkness to fight, he didn't need that mark on his soul too."

His words take me back, I can't say I'd ever considered any of what he just said, and I chide myself for keeping my rose-tinted glasses on for so long. I always looked at the situation with the eyes of a child. From my own selfish point of view, and everything I lost. Not once had I looked at it his way, like an adult making a decision with the least repercussions. I had always looked upon that day with the memory of the child I was, with the prejudices and opinions of a child, completely unwavering in my faith that he was in the wrong, and just playing his father's game, willing or not. My grief had clouded a lot, and my parent's grief had kept me distracted enough never to re-evaluate anything.

"I'm sorry, Cade."

"You don't need to be sorry, Emilia." He sighs and sits on the blanket in front of us.

"I do. I blamed you. For everything. I never considered anything outside of the black and white of what happened in front of me that day. I've been wearing rose-tinted glasses for quite some time, and so I'm sorry."

"Does that mean you forgive me? Rohan? My father?"

"I don't think I'll ever forgive your father, Cade. It might not be what you want to hear, and it might jeopardize my chances here with all of this, but I will be honest with you when you ask. Your father orchestrated that whole thing to test Rohan, to test you, he could have used anyone. A nobody. But he chose Edimere as his plaything, and for that, I will never forgive him. I lost more than Edi that day, and nothing anyone can say or do will ever be able to change that. Everything that happened since then has remolded me into someone I never thought I'd be, but it has made me stronger at least." I take a seat beside him, the basket between us. "But let's try and not focus on that, this is meant to be about us getting to know each other as we are now."

"I already know who you are, Emilia. All of you. Whether you want me to see it or not. You're still exactly who you've always been, even if you are a little more cautious now, a little more jaded. I, however, I've been lost ever since that day. I lost you, and I lost the part of me that you brought out in me. The part of me that wanted more than I'd been taught we should have. More than the old ways, and ever since you've been here, that part of me has been battling with the man I know I have to be. I'm not who I once was, I've learned hard lessons and lost so much of myself, what I wanted from life in the years we've been apart, and I'm not sure who to be or how to act around you anymore."

"I've changed a lot too, Cade. I don't expect anything from you, except to give me a fair chance, and for us to try and forget our past." He takes my hand, and I swallow the lump in my throat as Oberon's face flashes in my mind, and I feel a stabbing feeling in my heart. My emotions swirl inside of me, and the conflict I feel confuses me. I never thought I could move past Edimere's death, but being here, being back with Cade, is healing parts of me I thought would be forever broken. I've realized that holding onto that hate and bitterness will only hurt me, except that in letting go of that anger, something else has crept in. I'm not ready to look too closely at it because it could ruin everything. For now, I just need to make it through this and stay strong. I'm here for Oberon, and I can't forget that.

"I can do that if you can. A fresh start for us both, what do you say?" He hits me with that smile of his, and I can't help but smile back at him, feeling lighter than I have in a long, long time.

"That sounds perfect." I squeeze his hand as his fingers intertwine with mine, and I almost feel at peace. Now I just need to hold strong and stay on this path. Maybe I can be happy here, and save Oberon, and stop the brewing war with the Hunters all at the same time.

12

I stare at my ceiling and sigh, frustrated for the hundredth time about the fact that I can't get back to sleep. *Snap out of it, Emilia.*

Screw this. I throw off the covers and dress in the jeans and sweatshirt I'd put out for the morning. It might be stupid o'clock, but lying in bed isn't going to sort out any of my frustrations. I grab my jacket and leave my room, aimlessly wondering through the palace, and find myself outside.

I walk around the palace on edge, I've been so tense since Lily's visit, and I still haven't spoken to Cade about it. I don't know where to start or what he already knows, and I'm making myself crazy. But if what Lanora said is right, marrying Cade is going to bring about more death and darkness, but if I don't, then this war could go full-scale if my father kills Oberon. Either way, whichever decision I make, I'm guaranteed to lose, and so are the people I'm meant to rule and protect. A walk in the gardens is just what I need, the fresh air will help me sleep.

It's dark, and the quiet of the night makes the palace seem so eerie. I head back inside and walk through the halls, and find myself staring at the doors of the ballroom. Every bad thing that has happened to me in this place has happened beyond these doors. I push one open, the creak of it deafening in the silence. I step forward and slip, crashing to the floor. I feel the wet on my fingers, and then the smell hits me—blood.

I pull myself back up and creep into the room, trying not to disturb anything or anyone who might be in here already. I head down the stairs, crouching the best I can, and walk towards the smell. My foot slips and I catch myself of the bannister, looking down I see the blood trail, smeared on the floor. I follow the drag lines with my eyes, and I see them. Three or four bodies piled together. A groan sounds from the pile, and I rush towards them.

"Run… Hunters…" the man before me says, his breath gets shallow and ropey before stopping completely. *What the fuck is going on?*

That's when I see the shadows in the room moving, and I realize I'm not alone. I run back out the way I came and head for Cade, screaming his name as I run. I already know they're behind me, but maybe I can save him if he hears me. My blood pumps so hard through my body that

I can hear my heartbeat in my ears. I get close to the wing where Cade and Rohan stay when I'm thrown backwards by a rush of heat. I hit my head on the wall that stops me and fall to the floor. The brightness in front of me blinds me, and I scream. The flames engulf the main staircase up to the two wings. I pull on the power inside me and reach out to the flames. The ringing in my ears threatens to knock me off balance, but I stand and reach out for them, making sure I have them all inside my mind, and I extinguish them.

The damage done to the main area is extensive, but I'll be damned if that's going to stop me.

"Emilia, run!" I look up and see Cade and Rohan, both covered in soot and looking worse for wear, but at least they're alive. The fear on their faces registers as I feel the hand on my shoulder before I'm thrown backwards again. I shake myself off as I hit the floor and jump back up. Hell, if I'm going down without a fight.

"Get to your parents," I shout to Cade and Rohan as I face the smug smile and glowing yellow eyes of the Hunter in front of me. I hear their footfalls as they run to the other wings, trusting I can handle myself, and I love that feeling.

"We're not here for you, Emilia. Don't make yourself part of this. Run from here, find Oberon, and leave just as you planned." I hesitate.

"Oberon is free?" I whisper. This is it, the moment I wanted for so long, right in front of me.

"He will be by the time you get to the cages. Go. Go now. These are not your people, not really. This is not your fight." He turns and walks away from me, and I falter. Can I really leave knowing what could happen? Can I not?

I swallow the bad taste on my tongue, and I run without looking back. I make it out of the palace without seeing anyone else, but I look back and see the flames that engulf half of the palace, and I hear the cries of Hunters and Fae alike as they battle out in the palace, but I don't stop. Oberon is free. Once I reach the stables, I find most of them already empty. One lone black stallion remains, mounted and ready to go. Shadowind, Cade's horse, and the irony of the situation isn't lost on me, but I climb the horse and head back towards home. Towards the man I love. Towards freedom.

I try to stop the thoughts running through my head that this is a bad idea. Try to force the worry for Cade and Rohan down, I fear that I love them both too. It's not the same as my love for Oberon, but it's there, a small flame next to the inferno Oberon brings out in me. I reach the cliff point between the two courts, and I see the ice and flames battling as they engulf the Summer palace, and it hits me. They're not just attacking in one place. I bend over and throw up, the bile stinging my throat as it leaves my body. All these people, dead or dying because of me. Because I fell in love with a Hunter. Because we got caught. Tears stream down my face, and the hope I'd been running on is empty.

I head towards the spot where I said I'd meet Lily, I need to make sure she's safe before I find Oberon. I don't think I could handle it if anything happened to her. We climb the rocky road up the cliff to the high point between the two courts, I can't see anything but trees, but I can hear screams and the roar of fires, and I hope beyond hope that everyone I love is okay—even my parents.

I think back on leaving Cade and Rohan, their family, and it hits me. I love Cade too, more than the small flame of friendship I had thought it was. My stomach churns, and I feel like I'm going to be sick. How can I love two people? Be *in* love with two people? I dismount the horse and tie his reins to a close tree, then I sit to wait for Lily and play it all out in my head. Of course, I still love Oberon, don't I? Or do I just think I do because I should? Because loving Cade feels like a betrayal, yet I can't deny the thought of him being hurt, or worse, it makes my heart want to shrivel into dark nothingness. It makes me want to scream, the thought of him not being there, and I wonder why I left. Why didn't I realize this sooner? Of course, I still love Oberon, but our love was different. It was from a darker place of need and pain. But with Cade, it's not like that. We have history, but I loved him before all of the bad shit happened. He was the one who saved me time and again when I was younger, and he's tried to save me again now, and I repaid him by running. What have I done?

I look around for Lily and her family, but there is no sign of them. I worry my bottom lip between my teeth, the dilemma of what to do. My heart wants me to run back to the Winter Palace, back to Cade, but I also need to make sure Lily is okay. I take a deep breath and clear my mind. Lily has her father. I'm sure he'll get them out safely. I need to go back to the palace. I saw how bad it was there, they'll need my help. I turn to undo Shadowind's reins when I hear them coming, and I know it's too late for me to try to hide.

"Well lookie, lookie boys. We came across a damsel in distress, and a princess nonetheless," the Hunter in front of me taunts as the group of four with him snicker. "What should we do with such precious cargo?"

"Isn't she Oberon's?" one of the others asks, and the ringleader's face darkens.

"If she is, she's the reason he screams out each day and night. Maybe we should show her how that feels?"

"Not sure if I get much input here, but yeah. Totally not down for that," I say, and steady my stance, preparing to fight. It's been a long time since I fought anyone, and I've never fought a Hunter, but Erion's words ring out in my head. *Cover yourself and aim for the softest tissue. Eyes, ears, throat, so many sweet spots open to you Emilia. Use them and run. Your powers won't always save you.*

They creep closer, spreading out to surround me, and I reach inside myself to the fire that sits there. I may not have many gifts like some, but the one I have, I know inside and out. My hand lights, and they pause.

"Is this really the best idea? There might be five of you, and one of me, but I was sent here to find Oberon. He is waiting for me." I watch as they take in the information, but their ringleader just sneers at me. "I might not look like much, but you shouldn't underestimate me either." I call on my fire, wrapping it around me like a safety blanket.

"You've had your fun rolling around with the beast, but once we kill your precious family, and those Winter Royals you hold so dear, maybe you'll realize that you should have stuck to your own kind." He launches at me, and I dodge and throw a fireball in his direction before I'm grabbed by another. I push my flames into the Hunter who holds me, who howls out in pain before he lets me go. I need to get back to Cade. I can't let them hurt him.

"This isn't over yet, Princess." I look to the voice and realize this Hunter is a female, her bald head shines in the moonlight. "Oberon was one of the good ones, and you thought you could just take him?" She dives towards me, and I feel the ice before I can lift my hands, and it hits me square in the chest. I feel as it runs through my veins with every beat of my heart, pushing it further, rendering me useless. I fight it, pushing all of my energy into creating a wall of fire around her, she jumps back, nearly falling into the flames, it takes almost everything I have left to keep it going. I fall to my knees at the weight of the cold inside of me, the ice in my veins makes it agony to move, to breathe. I refuse to give up yet. I am not going out without a fight. I think about Cade, Lily, Rohan, and everyone else who has ever caused me to have love or hate in my heart and I use it, creating a blast of fire against the others who wanted to hurt me. I hear their screams, which I know will haunt me. It's not much, but it's all I have left to protect myself against whatever else they wanted to throw at me. My eyesight blurs as I feel the ice she put in my heart take hold, and I try not to let out a cry as my flames around her extinguish.

"Now, you'll feel what it's truly like to feel helpless." She smiles before raising her hand and brings it down against my cheek, it feels as if the bone splinters as she hits, knocking me to the ground. I hear laughter, and cry out as a foot hits my spine, thrusting me forward. I try to reach inside of me, to my fire, to thaw the ice in my bones, but it's dying under the icy assault that she shoots at me once again. The laughter rains down around me as they take it in turns to beat me, each laughing more as another bone breaks, or my skin splits, and I bleed onto the ground.

When I can barely take any more, they tie me up, and I'm powerless to fight against them. I hear movement in the trees, and that's when I see more Hunters—one carrying a body. They dump the body on the ground next to me, face down in the dirt.

"Toby, glad you could join us, and you brought a toy.

Ours is about done. Can't keep ours, though." The woman's voice laughs. She comes over and kicks the body on to its side, when I see her face. Lily.

"No, please, no. Leave her alone," I cry out with what little voice I have.

"Oh, even better, the princess cares about her. Maybe we should make her watch as we play with her little friend." She kneels down beside me and lifts my chin to meet her eyes, the point of her talon making me bleed where it digs into my skin. "Yes, I think that's exactly what we'll do."

I try to cry out as they wake her from whatever magical sleep they had her in, but my voice is almost gone.

"What the hell? Where am I? Who the hell are you?" Lily shouts as she fights against the Hunter holding her. The woman who was torturing me slaps her around the face, and I wince as I hear the crack.

"Shut up, you pathetic little Fae bitch. Fates, I might kill you quickly just to stop that squeaky voice of yours. Or I might kill you slowly, just to see how much you can take, how much your friend can take before she passes out." At her words, Lily notices me, broken and bleeding, their ropes somehow stopped me from healing, or it could just be the sheer amount of damage they caused.

"Emmy… What the fuck did you do to her?" she screeches and starts to struggle against the Hunter again. I've never felt so helpless in my entire fucking life. I struggle against the ropes, try to call on my fire, but my body is beyond beaten, and I have nothing left.

I helplessly watch as they bind her hands and ankles, and then hang her by her wrists from one of the trees lining the grove. The first guy who attacked me steps forward with a look of pure glee. He lengthens his talons and looks me directly in the eye before he cuts through her dress, leaving a trail of blood behind from the cuts he inflicts. Her screams shake me and I struggle harder against the ropes binding me. I feel one of them loosen and try to focus on that rather than the screams being ripped from my best friend. The woman crouches down beside me and pulls my head up by my hair.

"Just want to make sure you're enjoying the show," she says icily, laughing at herself. I swear if I get free of this, she will be the first to die. I keep working at the rope on my wrist, loosening it with each movement. I feel my wrist break free, and a rush of power fills me. I call my flames to the surface and press my hand against her face.

Her screams stop the Hunters torturing Lily and bring everyone rushing towards me. I send out streams of my fire, but there are so many of them now that with my diminished strength, they overwhelm me once again, raining down on me with their strength and power.

"Enough." I hear the female Hunter's voice ring out before another icy blast wreaks havoc on my bleeding and broken body. "We need to get to the meeting point, and if we stay any longer, we'll be late."

"Kill the girl," she barks, and the Hunter who carried Lily into the clearing walks over to her and slits her throat with his talons, while another rebinds my ropes. I can do nothing but watch as the blood pours out of Lily. Tears run down my face for my friend who deserved so much more from life than this.

Once the blood stops, they cut her bindings, and the one who arrived with her throws her over his shoulders and leaves. My sobs drown out most of their words, but I hear their mumbles continue and their footsteps as they walk away.

I retreat inside myself and try to reach out to Cade, though I know I don't have that power no matter how much I wished I did, just to tell him how sorry I am. To tell him how much I wanted to come back to him, and that I'm sorry that I ever left. I realize that I was wrong before and that in letting go of my anger, some of the reasons I loved Oberon, the selfish reasons, are gone now, and I cry at my own stupidity as the blackness engulfs me.

"Oh my god, Emilia." I hear the words and try to register the voice, but I can't open my eyes, the pain is too much. I slip back into the darkness where it's warm and lose myself.

13

I open my eyes and stretch out before I realize something isn't quite right. I don't hurt. I sit up, and the room spins a little, and I'm back in my room at the Winter Palace.

"Steady on there, Emilia, you need to rest." I look up and see Cybil smiling down at me sadly. I shake my head but try to stand.

"I need to see Cade." I steady myself on the bed frame, as she walks towards me and offers me an arm. "What's wrong?" I ask, she's being too nice.

"I… It's not my place to tell you. Let us go and find Master Cade." She sweeps the hair off my face and treats me with a soft smile, and the pit of my stomach churns with dread.

"Please tell me that everyone is okay?" She pats my hand and walks me out of the door.

"You need to speak to Master Cade. Let's go, just move slowly, you're still healing. They only brought you in early this morning.

We got the healers in to see to most of your injuries, but there were a lot. I've never seen... I'm just glad you're okay." She guides me out of the room and through the palace, letting me take in the destruction and havoc that was wreaked on it during the attack. I see soldiers moving bodies, both Fae and Hunter alike. Others are working magik to rebuild damage to the structure, but each person is playing their part, and I can't help but feel responsible and useless all at once. Guilt tars my tongue and I struggle to swallow. I can feel the grief pouring off of each and every person here, the weight of it on my shoulders. Cybil leads me up the partially rebuilt staircase and towards the library at the back of the boys' wing.

She pushes the door open softly, and we walk in, Cade and Lanora sit together, crying. They look up at the sound of us entering, and Lanora flies at me.

"This is all your fault!" she screams. "I told you it was coming, and you didn't listen. Why couldn't you just listen to me!"

"Mother, calm yourself." Cade places his hand on her arm, using his powers to steady her, and she calms instantly.

"I'm so... sorry. I didn't mean for any of this. How bad is it?" I ask around the lump in my throat. Cade hands

Lanora over to Cybil, who guides her out of the room, whispering quietly to her.

"We took a lot of hits last night, we lost people. A lot of people." His voice is hoarse, thick as he tries to keep his emotions in check. I take in his red-rimmed eyes, his tired appearance, and the redness of the skin on his arm.

"I'm sorry... I..." I try to find the words to tell him about Lily, but I can't find it in me to say it. It's too fresh, too raw.

"Have you seen a healer, Cade?" I gesture to his arm, and he tugs at the sleeve of his shirt.

"I have more important things to deal with right now, plus you needed them more than I did." His voice shakes, so I take his hand and make him sit with me.

"What happened, Cade? What happened after I saw you?"

"It's my fault, I was distracted... I wasn't paying attention. There was so much blood, Emilia. It was on my hands. I lost myself last night, fighting them, tearing through them to try and save him. But I was too late. I hesitated." He cradles his head in his hands and falls into my lap, so I stroke his hair.

"This is not your fault, Cade. No one saw something like this coming."

"I should have known. We should've been more prepared, but they turned on us, and now... so many people lost their lives because I wasn't ready."

"Who did you lose, Cade?" I ask, not wanting the answer, as my blood runs cold with fear.

"They cut his throat while they held me down Emilia. I couldn't move, I couldn't fight. Their strength, I wasn't strong enough. My mother's screams will haunt me for the rest of my life. I don't want to say the words. I don't want this to be real. I'm not ready for this."

"I'm here, Cade. We'll get through this together. We can get through any of it." My words hold more strength than I feel, but I can feel the fine line he's walking, and with his mother lost, I need him to keep it together, even if just for now.

"They killed my father, Emilia. The gutted him like an animal. He was drugged, under some kind of spell, unable to fight back. Those cowards! I felt the spray of it on my face as they cut into him, I can still feel it, replaying inside my mind. Rohan and I tried to fight back, but it was useless. Rohan got free, and he ran for Talia and Arabella, but they didn't make it either. The soldiers arrived and pushed the Hunters back, but it was too late. They were already gone."

"Rohan... he's gone?" I can barely utter the words.

"No, Rohan is injured, but he will be okay soon enough."

"Cade, I am so sorry," I say as tears stream down my face. "This isn't your fault, it's mine. It's all my fault."

"There was nothing you could have done, Emilia." He

holds me tight, and guilt snakes around my heart when he comforts me, when it was his father that died, and it's because of my family. Because of me.

"Cade, I need to tell you something."

"There is nothing you need to worry about Emilia, this was not your fault. The entire time you were gone, I was losing my mind, even with everything else I should have been focusing on, all I could think about was you, and if you were safe. It made me realize I can't be without you, Emilia. You mean more to me than I ever thought possible, and when Erion brought you back to us, I died a little, thinking you might not make it. This is probably the worst time possible to say anything, in fact I know it is, but I can't wait any longer…"

A knock interrupts him as the door opens, and Cybil returns with a sorry smile.

"Your majesty, your father's council are asking for you. To arrange your coronation, the funerals, and our retaliation."

"Thank you, Cybil, have them gather in the war room, I'll be down shortly." She nods and leaves us again, and my words are stuck in my throat. I don't know if I can tell him.

"They attacked the Summer Court too," I tell him and wait for the realization to hit him. "We can face the Hunters together and bring our courts together to do so. This isn't all on you, Cade. You need to take the time to heal, to grieve." I wince at my words, knowing I have more to say.

"I can't do this without you, Emilia. Any of it. I was going to tell you today, I had it all planned out, but then all of this happened, but I picked you. My parents knew, I told them last night, before… You make me stronger, you keep me grounded, and you make me want to be a better man. A better king. We can rule together and face this new enemy side by side." I feel myself pale at his words. I'm not ready for this, and I can't do this. Not now. Not until he knows everything. It doesn't matter how much I love him, he only thinks he loves me because he doesn't know, and that thought terrifies me.

"They're going to do my coronation in two weeks after we rebuild and bury our dead. We will have time to plan everything, and I want you there by my side. I'll show you how to enjoy all of the darkness, show you we're just swimming in the stars of the sky, not drowning in the shadows that grip us, and try to drag us down. I've never felt like this before, and I want you with me every step for the rest of our lives."

I stand and take a step away from him. He's never going to understand.

"Tell me you'll be here when this is done, Emilia. That we can talk, that we can move forward together."

"I can't… There is more you don't know, Cade. I can't do this with secrets between us, it's going to bury us both. But once you know, you might not even want me like that anymore, and I'm scared. I don't want to lose what we've only just got back."

"I'm not going anywhere, Emilia. I've lost too much already. The thing that haunted me the most after everything that happened was all the things I'd never said to you. And with everything that's happened, it's glaringly obvious to me how short life can be, and how things out of our control can change everything, so I need to tell you now everything I never said. How I really felt, how I really feel about you."

"And how do you feel about me, Cade?" He kisses me and steals my breath. His hands are in my hair as he cradles me close and kisses me like his life depends on it. But it's not hard or rushed. It's soft, teasing, but devouring. He pulls back, and I finally see the man I loved for years when I was younger looking back at me, telling me everything I used to want to hear.

"I can't do this without you, Emilia, we've already been apart for so long, but you make me want to be better. If it's my decision to make, then I pick you. I want you to be my wife, to lead at my side and be my queen." My stomach drops, and I catch my breath. I feel the exact moment I fall in head over heels in love, deeper down the rabbit hole than I ever thought I could go, with Cade Vasara, and the exact moment my heart breaks because I know I can't marry him, not when I'm the reason his father is dead.

"I can't." I run from the room and hit a wall of muscle.

"I'm so sorry. I wasn't looking…"

"Emilia, thank God you're okay!"

"Erion? Is that… is that really you?"

14

"*J*s that really you?" I ask. I reach forward to touch him and wonder if I'm losing my mind.

"Hello, baby sister," he says softly before wrapping me up in a giant bear hug. "You're looking better today."

"I'm... You're... I'm so confused. How are you here?" I can't believe he's really here, that he's real. It feels like forever since I saw him, and I feel tears fill my eyes.

"How about we go somewhere a bit more private than this? We have a lot to catch up on." He gestures to the hall around us, and all of the Fae watching us. I nod and grab his hand, pulling him through the corridors to my room.

Once I close the door, I hug him again, just to make sure he's real. My emotions are already running high, but seeing him, it breaks the dam inside me, and I start to cry. "I'm so glad you're really here."

"You're okay, Em. I'm here now."

"How are you here?" I pull back from him and let him lead me to the chairs by the windows.

"I got a letter from Cade yesterday telling me to go home, along with a Royal pardon from any more time in the services. I was pissed at first and confused as hell, but I took it for the pardon it was and got the hell out of dodge, except I walked out of one war zone into another. I was on the main road to get home when I found you. I thought you were dead, Em. I've never felt so much panic in my entire life. I had no idea what to do, but then I saw Cade's horse, he's had Shadowind forever, and so I brought you here. I still have no idea why you're here, but when I arrived with you in my arms this morning, even with the devastation, people jumped to get you and make you better. I've missed a lot, huh?" I laugh and wipe the tears that continue to run down my face.

"You could say that, but you're here now, and that's what is important. I am so, so happy you're here. I thought you were lost to us, but you still seem like you."

"I'm changed, but I'm still the brother you remember, Em. I've just managed to work through a lot of the pain and anger I had when I signed up. War will do that to a guy. And look at you now, all grown up. You're beautiful, Em. I wish Edimere were still here too, so we could've seen the man he would've become."

"Me too," I say, the lump in my throat thick. "It's been so hard sometimes, Erion. I've wished you'd come home a thousand times over. I even tried to come find you once, but no one would help me. I've been so lost, and I missed my big brother. You always knew just what to say or what to do, and I was just floundering out here on my own. I'm just so glad you're here now."

"I can't change any of it, Em, but I wished I was home a thousand times too. Seeing the things I saw, some of them I will never be able to forget. And I'm sorry I left you. Now, why don't you tell me why you're here instead of home, not going to lie, my mind was completely boggled when I saw you with that damn horse."

"Oh, Erion, I don't even know where to start. So much happened after you left…" I slowly fill him on how things changed with our parents after he left, about wanting to run away, about Oberon, and about father's threats that led me to be living in the Winter Palace. I tell him about finding forgiveness, in finding the friendships I thought were lost to me forever, about letting go of all of the pain that weighed me down, and finally starting to fall for Cade again.

"I know it's probably not what you wanted to hear, but I do love him. Except before you just found me, he asked me to marry him, and I said no. He doesn't know about why I came here, and I know it's going to ruin everything, Erion. And now his father is dead." Erion stands and pulls me close, hugging me again, a tear running down his face that he swipes away.

"I am so sorry I left, Emilia. I'm sorry that I left you to

deal with all of this alone. I didn't consider that you'd be losing us all when we lost Edimere. I was so angry and so full of pain, I just wanted to escape. I hope you can forgive me one day too."

"Oh, Erion, I never faulted or blamed you for leaving. I knew you were dealing the only way you could, I just missed you so, so much!" A knock sounds, and my door opens, and a bashful Rohan enters before I can say anything.

"Hey, you guys. I figured I'd find you in here."

"Rohan? Look at you all grown up," Erion says, I can't hear any trace of anger or blame in his voice, and I relax even further.

"I could say the same about you. Welcome home, I'm glad you made it back safe, and thank you for bringing Emilia back to us."

"Thank you for fixing her up. Get in here, man." Erion walks to the door and hugs Rohan, who looks like he just got his long-lost brother back. "I'm sorry about your old man too," Erion says, hugging him just a bit tighter before stepping back.

"Thanks, I'm not sure it has sunk in yet. There's just so much, and Mother has had to be sedated again. I'm sure it'll hit me soon enough."

"I'm so sorry, Rohan." I fling myself at him and squeeze him tight, and I think he knows I'm apologizing for more than just Earon being gone. "It's all my fault, and then I left…"

"I don't blame you, Em. You're in a situation of your father's making. I've been there. I don't hold any grudges against you."

"He knows?" Erion asks, and I nod. "Well then, I guess I owe you extra thanks, but you know your brother is going to be pissed when he finds out, right?"

"When I find out what?" Cade walks through the door, with little Erion, and my eyes go wide.

"Cade, I don't know if now is the right time…"

"There's not going to be a better one, Emilia," he says before he whispers to little Erion. Cade kneels and puts little Erion on the floor while looking up at my brother. "It has been a long time, old friend."

"That it has," Erion says and holds out his hand, while eyeing up the child beside Cade. "And who is this little guy?"

"My name is Erion," he says, "and I'm four!"

My brother looks around the room at each of us, confused. "That's a cool name, buddy. It's mine too!"

"Really? My daddy has our name too. He's a hero, fighting the bad guys and keeping us all safe. Isn't that right Uncle Cade?"

"That's right, Erion." Cade's voice cracks as he watches my brother's face come to recognition.

"Is he…?" My brother looks from Cade to Rohan to me, and I nod. I kneel down to little Erion and take his hand.

"Do you remember me saying my brother's name was

the same as your daddy's?" He nods at me slowly, not quite understanding what's going on. "Well, this Erion is my big brother, but he's also your daddy."

I watch as his eyes light up, his confusion gone. "Daddy?" He rushes to my brother and jumps into his arms. "I've missed you so much!"

Tears fall down my face as I watch my shell-shocked brother crumple.

"I missed you too. I'm so sorry I wasn't here before now." His voice cracks as he goes to his knees.

"That's okay, Daddy, Uncle Cade and Uncle Rohan kept me safe and taught me all sorts of cool stuff when Mommy was busy or at work or poorly."

"Thank you," he says to Rohan and Cade. "I can't even… Thank you."

"Why don't we go find your mama, Erion?" Rohan suggests, and little Erion jumps up.

"Okay. Don't go away again, please, Daddy. I missed you too much."

"I'm not going anywhere, son," he tells him, letting him go slowly. He watches until they leave the room, and Rohan shuts the door.

"I have a son," he says, falling back and sitting on the floor. "This has been the fucking most insane twenty-four hours ever."

"I didn't know how to tell you," I tell him softly.

"Who is his mother?" he asks nobody in particular.

"The redhead from the dance team who came to visit the soldiers about four years ago?"

"You mean Sarah? Oh, my fucking god. Why did nobody tell me?" he shouts.

"We tried," Cade tells him. "And when we got nothing back, we tried your parents, and when that failed, I took him under my wing. You were like a brother to me once upon a time, it seemed only right."

"Thank you, Cade. I know we probably need to talk, but I can't thank you enough. If I'd have known…"

"I know, but honestly, I was happy to. He kept a little piece of me alive when the rest of me turned cold. He's probably done more for me than I have for him. It was an honor. But I'm not here with entirely happy news."

"What happened?"

"The attack on the Summer Court… I'm sorry, Emilia, but I just got news that Lily was caught up in it. She was found this morning, and it was too late to help her."

"I know, I was there. They… They made me watch." I crumble, and Erion catches me. The tears come again, refreshed. I'm not sure how many more people I can survive losing. He holds me while Cade crouches down in front of us.

"Emilia, I know you're angry, and you're sad, and you have every right to be, god knows I am, but we have things to do before we can grieve properly. And Erion, I know you've only just returned from one war, but we could really use your input on defense systems, tactics—you know the deal. We lost a lot of people last night pushing the Hunters back. The rest of the troops on both sides have called a cease-fire and are heading home."

"Do you mind?" he says to Erion, who shakes his head.

"I won't be far if you need me, Em. I'm going to find Rohan, and my… my son." He gulps, and I stand with the help of Cade. Erion hugs us both again quickly before leaving us alone again.

"I think we need to talk, Emilia." I nod and sit back down on the floor. Maybe down here it won't hurt so much when he leaves me on the floor crying, because I don't see this conversation going any other way.

"What was it that was going to make me pissed?" I look up at him, his pain apparent in his every movement, every word, every sigh, and I know I can't lie to him anymore.

"I am here because of my father. He imprisoned the man I loved, and his offer was that I come here and do my duty, and that man I loved would go free." I feel his pain as I say the words, and I know I've broken his heart all over again. "I regret it, all of it. Choosing the life of one over many, but I know that the attack would've happened regardless, because either way, my father either captured a Hunter or killed one. They were going to come for us, and I didn't see it coming. I wish I had, I wish I could change all of this, but this is where we are."

"You never really forgave me, did you? Forgave any of us? This has all been one big lie. It's nothing more than a game for you, is it?" he roars, and I don't think he even notices the tears on his cheeks.

"That's why I came here, Cade. It's not why I stayed. I was free, the palace was under siege, and I escaped. I could've stayed gone, been a victim of it all, lost to the battle, but I didn't. I came back!"

"You were rescued, how am I meant to know that you stayed for me, and not because you had no other choice? You left here for that monster, and now my father is dead, your friend is dead, because of his kind. You abandoned us for him. How am I meant to trust anything you say? That you're not here to spy for him."

"If you think that, you're an even bigger idiot than I ever thought you could be! Erion bought me back here, and I've not seen him since the day after Edimere died. Even with your grief, surely you see it. You feel it? I am so sorry about your father, Cade. Truly I am, and if I could change it and take away your pain, I would, but please don't doubt how I feel. You can read my emotions, we both know that you can, so read the truth of my words. Do it. Feel it. Stop locking yourself away from me, stop shutting me out and just let me in." I reach forward and pull him towards me, his forehead against mine, and I make him see, really see the truth inside of me.

"Oberon and my father might be the reasons I ended up here, Cade, but you and Rohan were the reasons I stayed. I see you, the you that you keep locked away. The you your father taught you to be isn't who you really are. The man I knew back then was kind, he was forgiving, and he'd protect those he loved fiercely. That's the man I fell in love with all those years ago, that's the man I catch glimpses of, and that's why I stayed, why I tried to get back to you even while I was dying on the ground, taking the worst beating I've ever known. It gave me hope, knowing that the man I used to know was still here. I thought what you did, when you killed him, that you'd disappeared alongside Edimere, but now I see you're right here, even though you're hiding under your grief and your anger. I'm not afraid to fight for you. I would take on the world for the man that I know you are. It may have taken us a lot to get here, but we *are* here, and now we have the opportunity to change everything. We can be those people we wanted to be, as long as we do it together. Don't you see? But I don't want what's happened to change all of this. Everything we've been heading towards."

"Do you really believe that?" I look at him properly, and that's when I see it. The fear. The grief. The confusion.

"What I've learned is that people will do outrageously stupid things for the people we love. You lost a lot that day too, I can see that now. Who knows what might have happened one day if Edimere were still here? What I said, I believe it with everything I am, Cade. But I need you to forgive me too. We can't do any of this with our pasts hanging over us. Both of our fathers put us in situations out of our control, and the repercussions are devastating."

"So why did you say nothing when I asked you to be my queen? To be my *wife*. You had the chance to tell me then, to explain.*"*

"I was scared, and I was punishing myself. I said no for this exact reason, Cade, this is what I feared. There were still too many secrets between us, there still is, and I don't want either of us to regret this. Do I wish I could change things? Take them back and redo them? Of course, I do, I'd give anything to give you your father back. I know that pain, and I wouldn't wish it on my worst enemy. But I also don't, because we found a way back to each other Cade, and that means more to me than you can imagine. That we're here, that we might even have this chance to explore what we could be, even shrouded in as much tragedy as it is. Rohan wants this for us, and he knows. He knows everything, and he still loves me and wants this for us. He is our biggest champion. Please don't let this break us apart when we worked so hard to reach this point. I can't lose you too."

"I don't want this to break us apart either, Emilia. I love you more than I ever thought it possible to love another person." He sweeps me into his arms and kisses me like his life depends on it, like my kiss is his oxygen, and I kiss him back because he is my life, my heart, the reason for me to keep fighting for our tomorrows.

"You will be my wife, Emilia. I'm not asking you

again now, not until it's right. But it's going to happen. It is going to feel right. Like it was always fated to be. Maybe not today or tomorrow, but one day soon it will hit you, exactly how it hit me. You'll see."

15

*T*wo days have passed since I saw Cade, and I still have no idea what is going on because people are treating me as if I don't exist, as if I can't help, and it's driving me fucking insane. So today, I'm determined to put a stop to it, and I'm going to be useful. I pull on my cloak over my jeans and jumper, and secure it tight before sneaking through the corridors of the palace until I reach fresh air.

Winter is officially here, and the powdery snow covers every surface. I walk in the quiet stillness, a contrast to inside the palace as they prepare for Cade's coronation, and what I can only imagine is another war. As I reach the stables, I hear Shadowind whinny.

"Oh, hey boy," I murmur as I stroke his strong neck. "You fancy playing hooky with me again?" He whinnies again, and I take that as his approval. I untie the rope on the stable door and grab his reins, walking him outside. I mount him quickly, and we gallop away, trying to escape before someone stops us. It doesn't take long to reach my destination, but the devastation I find down in the main city is horrific. So many people are still crying in the street, trying to rebuild after the devastation the Hunters left in their wake. There are still bodies waiting to be collected, there are pyre wagons lining the street, with bodies waiting for a funeral, lined with flowers and personal touches. My heart aches for all of the lives lost, and this is just the main city, I just hope the havoc hasn't reached farther towns. I climb off of Shadowind and secure his reins in the fence of a nearby garden before exploring further into the city.

The sadness and sorrow linger in the air, so bitter I can almost taste it, so thick it almost chokes me. I walk through the streets, keeping the hood on my cloak up, taking in the devastation from my decisions.

"Has anyone seen Callum? Please! Has anyone seen my son?" I watch on as a young woman clutches a picture as she works her way from person to person in the street. I feel her panic as she flits through the people. She reaches me and grasps my hands, and the breath is pulled from my body.

I see nothing but darkness, wisps of smoke. Screams ring out all around me. I move forward, gliding through the darkness... whispers reach out to me but I can't hear them fully. They tease me further into the darkness, pulling me deeper into the shadows. I stumble, tipping forward, but manage to steady myself. Kneeling, I look down into the hole before me, and I see them. All of them. The people reaching towards me, screaming for me to save them. Their faces blur, and I feel the cold sweep over me.

"The Hunt is coming…"

"Let go of me!" the woman screams in my face, and pulls out of my grasp, her arms bloody from where my nails dug into her skin.

"I am so sorry!" I move towards her, but she steps back from me, afraid. "I didn't mean to hurt you."

"What was that?" she looks at me, eyes wide.

"I… I don't know what you mean." I stutter. I go quickly back to Shadowind, and ride back to the palace.

"Emilia, are you okay? We've been looking for you everywhere!" Cade strides towards me, his face solemn.

"I'm sorry, I didn't mean to scare anyone, I just needed some air." I drop to the floor and pass Shadowind back to the stable hand. "I just needed to think. I went down to the city, it's so terrible down there, Cade."

"I know, but we will fix it, and the Hunters will be punished for their actions. Are you sure you're okay? You're so pale." I contemplate telling him, but I don't even know what happened.

"I'm fine." I shake my head. "Just not made for this kind of cold."

"Let's get you inside and by a fire. There is much to do for the coronation."

I should feel more excited at the prospect of a wedding, even if Cade hasn't asked me again yet but I know he will. It's just that with everything else happening around us, I can't help but feel like this is wrong.

"Cade, we need to talk," I call out to him from my chair in the corner of the library. The Palace has finished being pieced back together, and I've sat here while he has commanded people to various parts of his lands to secure the borders, and to help rebuild.

"What's wrong?" He takes my hand and sits opposite me.

"I think this is too much, too quick. We have so much we need to do, so many people need things from us. I think we need to wait with the wedding. I just… It doesn't feel right."

"I didn't ask you again yet," he says with a smirk, but then he sees the look on my face, and his smile falls. "You don't want to marry me? After all of this?"

"That isn't what I'm saying. Not at all. It took us a long way to find each other again, it just feels like we're rushing this, all of it. It doesn't feel like it's because it's what we want, but because we have to. Imagine if all of this hadn't happened. We'd have time. Time to find each other. Explore each other. But everything is because we have to. I'm not ready, Cade."

"Well, maybe it's because you're not really in love with me. I thought we'd finally gotten to a place where we could be happy, Emilia. Maybe you need to think about what it is that you finally want now that your parents aren't hanging threats over your head. You need to decide what you really want, and if it's me, come find me. If it's not, well, then we'll cross that bridge when we get there." He stands and storms from the room, leaving me alone with nothing but the noise of the crackling fire. I crawl into a ball, and I let it all out finally. The tears for Oberon, the tears for Lily, the pain of the fact that my parents didn't love me enough to sacrifice me. And now this. I cry until there are no tears left, and I fall asleep alone once again.

I startle awake, my fire tickling my fingertips. I feel as the pressure on my shoulder stops, and I see Rohan jump backwards.

"I didn't mean to scare you, Em. Sorry. You just didn't look very comfortable. My brother's been storming around like someone broke his favorite toy all afternoon, so I thought if I could find you, you could calm him down. I tried, but he froze my feet in place and told me to mind my own fucking business." He rolls his eyes, and I offer him a small smile.

"I'm not sure I'm the best person to help."

"Of course, you are!" he says, but then he looks at me properly and he groans, falling into the chair opposite me. "You guys are going to be the goddamn death of me! What happened now?"

"I told him it was too fast. I just keep watching as all of these things happen to me and are decided for me, but I feel lost. Like I didn't really get to pick any of this for myself, and what all of this has shown me is that life is fleeting, even for those of us who live as long as we do. We are not immortal, despite what the humans and their tales depict. We can die. And I don't want my life just to happen. I want to be able to look back and say I really lived. There are so many chains that come with our birthrights, but right now—right now I finally have the chance to be free. To live just for me. If I marry Cade without really thinking about it, I lose all of that. That chance to be free."

"I can understand that. Freedom is the mistress we all chase, even at the cost of those around us. But what you need to ask yourself, Emilia, and I mean really ask yourself, is if freedom is worth it. Is it worth the cost of love? What good is freedom if you're miserable? What good is seeing and experiencing all the things this life has to offer if you don't have someone to share them with? My brother loves you, probably enough to let you go if he thought that was really what you wanted. You just need to tell him."

He stands and kisses my cheek before leaving me alone in the quiet darkness again, and I contemplate his words.

What have I done?

I find myself out at the stables again, brushing down Shadowind. There is something about this horse that calms me like nothing else. It's so peaceful in here with him.

"I'm sorry, I didn't think you'd be here," Cade says on the other side of the stall. He scratches the back of his neck while he waits for me to respond, as I finish brushing Shadowind.

"It's okay. He's your horse. I just like the peace he brings me."

"He does the same for me." He opens the door and joins me in the stable. He starts stacking the hay, and we work in silence for a while, but it feels comfortable. Like Shadowind is the bridge between us, bringing us back to each other.

"I'm—"

"You—"

We laugh, shyly, and Cade takes a seat on one of the hay bundles.

"You go first," I tell him, and get comfortable on the bench behind me, as Shadowind lays on the floor between us with a quiet whinny.

"I'm sorry," he says with his head lowered. "I got so caught up in everything, I forgot to take a step back and take a breath. There are so many people that want and need so much from me right now, and I forgot to think about what I want and need. What *we* want and need."

"I'm sorry I didn't explain things better. I know how much pressure there is on you to do the right thing. To have all of the answers. Be the one everyone else can rely on. It's why I've barely seen you the last few days. But I don't want my life to be like that. Locked away, not seeing you days on end while you're off saving the world as we know it. I want more than that. I want adventure. I want to see the worlds. Explore all of the things the realms have for us. I don't want to do it alone, but I don't want to give up the freedom I've only just got in my grasp, Cade. I can't." He stands and walks over to me, kneeling on one knee in front of me.

"And I wouldn't ask you to, Emilia. I want all of those things too. I don't want you to be my wife because you should be. I want you to be my wife because you, my love, are the girl who bewitched my heart from the very moment I saw you. The girl who broke my heart when she walked away without a word. But you're also the woman who brought me back to myself. You helped me see again, you freed me. I would never ask you to give up your passions, because that would be me asking you not to be you."

I jump up and wrap my arms around his neck, and kiss him with everything I have, knocking us to the ground in the process.

"You are so beautiful, Emilia." He kisses me, and I don't care that I'm lying on a dirty floor in a stable, because I finally have everything I ever wanted. We've come a hell of a long way to get here. I lose myself in Cade's kiss, forget everything but the feel of his weight on top of me, his lips on mine. He pulls away, stands, and puts his hand out to me, pulling me to stand. He smiles as he plucks straws of hay from my hair before going back down on one knee and looking up at me.

"I didn't do this right the first time, but I'm no fool, so I won't do it again. You, Emilia, are the light to my dark, the warm to my cold, the fire to my ice. I can't imagine another day where we don't belong to each other, and so I ask. Will you be with me for the rest of existence? As my queen, but most importantly, as the other half of me. As my wife." I gasp as he pulls the ring box from his trouser pocket and gifts me the most beautiful ring I've ever seen. I nod as he slides the pink and white band down my finger, and I marvel as the blue stone glitters in the firelight.

"It's beautiful." I sigh.

"You are," he says before he kisses me again. He touches his forehead to mine, and I feel the heat coming from him, matched by the fire in his eyes. Wordlessly he takes my hand and leads me back to the palace.

The smoke chokes me as I try to get out. Where am I? I can't see through the smoke, and the roar of the flames fills my ears. I reach for my power to try and dull the flame, but it's not there. Why isn't it there? What is going on? I cough again as the smoke burns my throat and lungs. I drop to the floor to try to see and crawl around aimlessly, hoping to find a way out.

I reach out and feel another hand. I pull on it, hoping to find someone to help me, but I see Cade on the floor, his eyes and ears bleeding. I can't tell if he's breathing. Please, god, let him be breathing. I keep crawling, trying to pull him with me.

"You'll never save everyone," a deep voice resonates in my head, I recognize it, but I can't place it. The lack of oxygen makes me fuzzy. "You are the last one. The only one who could have done anything, but look at you. You're pathetic." The voice laughs, and I push harder to find its source, to find a way out.

I hit a wall and find a handle. Pushing as hard as I can, I fall through it, scrambling to bring Cade with me. I feel the fresh air on my face and suck it in.

"You never did deserve him. Any of them," the voice calls out before silencing, and I focus on Cade. He's not breathing. I push on his chest and breathe air into his lungs. Please don't leave me. Not now. Not yet. I keep pushing, but he isn't moving.

Emilia

I scream out, this can't be happening. Rage courses through me.

Emilia!

I let go and feel the anger swallow me whole.

"Emilia, wake up!"

I jolt up and look into Cade's eyes, gulping in air. I lunge forward and hug him.

"Hey, it's okay. It was just a bad dream," he soothes as he strokes my hair. The door bursts open, and Rohan rushes in, looking flustered.

"What is going on in here? I heard screams." I hide my face in the crook of Cade's neck and hide the redness climbing up my chest and face.

"We're all good, little brother, just a bad dream." Cade continues to stroke my hair, and while I know I should climb out of his lap, it feels so good.

"Glad to see you two made up," he chuckles, and then I hear the door shut again. I climb off Cade and scoot back against the pillows.

"Well, that wasn't too embarrassing or anything." I hide my face in my hands, *oh my god.*

"It's fine, Em. It's not like he's not an adult. Plus, he knew what I was asking you earlier. How do you think I found you?" Cade smiles and comes to sit beside me, wrapping an arm around my shoulders, tucking me into his side. His bare skin against mine is so cool, but strangely, it feels good.

"What were your nightmares about?"

"I… I—" I falter, and I realize I don't want to tell him. It seems so silly, but I don't want him to think I'm being negative about what we've just started. "I don't really remember. I just remember being scared and angry. I'm sure it was just something silly."

He looks at me with concern etched on his features, his stare unwavering, before he tucks me back under his arm and kisses the top of my head. "Nothing bad is going to happen to you now, Emilia. Not if I have anything to do with it."

"I don't know what to do, Emilia." Cade sighs with frustration. "She's my mother, but since she's lost her husband, she's losing her goddamn mind. She keeps screaming at people, she attacked Lex yesterday, and today she drew a blade on one of the healers I sent in to calm her. I'm running out of ideas." He runs his hands through his hair again, and I hate that I'm keeping her secret from him. I don't want any secrets between us, but I don't want to be the one to burden him with yet another thing he can't control.

"Have you tried speaking to her?" I squeeze his hand and let him know that I'm here for him.

"I've tried. Her babble is incessant. I don't think she even knows what she's talking about half the time. Rohan found an elixir to calm her mind, but I think she's just getting worse. I hate feeling this clueless, this helpless. And I can't show anyone but you how I'm truly feeling since everything is so precariously balanced right now."

"I'm sorry this is all happening, Cade. It's all my fault. My parents…" He puts a finger against my lips and quietens my shame.

"This is not your fault, Emilia. You were a pawn in the power play your parents made, all you ever did was love, and want to be loved. You didn't make the Hunters rebel. You didn't push them over the edge of the cliff. I don't want to hear this again. I need you to believe the truth of it all. None of this is because of you." I nod my head, not truly believing his words.

"But that doesn't fix the problems with your mother. Maybe I could try to speak with her?" I offer.

"You can try, maybe it'll do her good seeing someone who isn't trying to force her chatter to make sense."

"I'll visit her tonight, after our dinner with your brother and Lex." I roll my eyes.

"I know you don't like him, and I know you've had issues, but I've spoken to him. He was trying to look out for me, and he didn't think you were in my best interests. He is a good guy, deep, *deep* down. You just have to break through the bearish exterior." He walks over to me and wraps his arms around my waist, hitting me with his megawatt smile.

"Uh-huh, if you say so. I'm never going to be his biggest fan, but if he's your friend, despite everything, I won't burn him to ash."

"That would be good, considering he's going to be at the wedding…" I slap his arm and pull out of his embrace.

"Do I get a say in this at all? I'm all for playing nice at a dinner but it's my wedding day too, Cade, and the guy choked me. My neck was bruised for days. You'll have to forgive me for not being all rainbows and sunshine about this," I huff.

"Of course, you get a say, but there is going to be a lot of people there. Whether we want it or not, both courts are going to be joined with this wedding, and that means both courts will want to attend. That also means your parents."

"Pfft, I've not heard from my parents for a long time. They didn't even check in with me after the attack."

"Did you check in with them? Has Erion?"

"Erion has barely left the palace since the attack, he's either been here helping rebuild, or he's been with his son, trying to make up for lost time. I think considering my parents ignored the fact that he had a son, means he's ignoring the fact he has parents."

"Well, that's going to make for a fun surprise on our wedding day."

"I was thinking of asking him to walk me down the

aisle…" I chew my lip just thinking about it. I haven't dared approach him about it yet.

"Why are you worried?" He rubs up and down my arms, trying to soothe me.

"Just because of everything… Do you think he will?"

"I think he'd be devastated if you asked anyone else."

Well, dinner was exhausting, and my face hurts from the fake smile I plastered on the entire time. The only winning part was that Erion and Jnr joined us. I just left the boys to their war games, after little Erion was whisked away to bed, and now I'm slowly making my way towards Lanora's rooms. It's not that I don't want to see her, but the last time I did didn't exactly go so well. Plus, I have no idea if seeing me will help. She probably blames me for her husband's death and is going to go bat shit crazy at me, but I will try for Cade.

I knock on her door, and gently push it open, watching as she waters and trims the flowers in here.

"Lanora? Are you okay? It's me, Emilia." I slowly enter the room, not wanting to startle her, especially with the secateurs in her hands.

"Lanora?" She continues to work as if she can't hear me, so I continue to approach slowly, from the side, hoping she'll see me.

"Oh, hello, Emilia. I didn't hear you. What are you doing here?"

"I wanted to talk to you, I know I haven't been to visit much recently, and I'm sorry, we've been busy, but that's no excuse." She eyes me warily before taking a few steps back.

"I can see the darkness in you… it's taking hold!"

"Lanora, I'm not sure what you mean. Why don't we sit and talk? About the wedding, Cade's coronation. We have a lot to catch up on." Each step I take towards her, she takes another one back, so I stop moving. I don't want her to hurt herself anymore.

"You've seen it haven't you?" she whispers, looking around the room as if watching the shadows. "The Hunt is coming for us. The Hunters must have called on it to help them. We need to stop it before it reaches here. Before it takes us all."

"I don't know what you mean." Her words shake me. I don't want to think about what I've been seeing. How could she possibly know?

"There is much I need to tell you, child. I do not know how you saw, but I can sense it. I saw it too. The Wild Hunt comes for us all."

"But the Wild Hunt is nothing more than a scary story we tell children at night, it isn't real."

"The Wild Hunt has been dormant for centuries, locked away by our ancestors when we drew an alliance with the humans, but it is real enough. I don't know how they unleashed it, or even if they have succeeded yet, but the darkness is coming."

"The Hunters have gone into hiding, and despite all of our trackers, magical and otherwise we cannot find them. They have masked themselves. The Wild Hunt isn't real, Lanora. Why don't we sit you down, and calm down with a cup of tea?"

"Do not mock me, child. I know what I have seen. There is so much you do not know, and I shouldn't be the one to tell you. You and I are more alike than you know, and I sympathize with all you've been through, but we need you now, more than we've ever needed you. I need you to remember." She paces in the room, staring at the ceiling as she continues to mumble.

"Remember what, Lanora? What on earth are you on about?" I try to encourage her to sit again, but she pushes me away and screams.

"You will be the end of us all! You must remember. The darkness is coming. The darkness is coming!" she screams in my face, her eyes turning white before she falls to the ground, lifeless.

"Lanora!" I dive towards her as her door crashes open, and the medical team swarm in. Cade, Rohan, and Lex follow quickly behind, and Cade grabs me out of the way.

"I'm so sorry Cade. I just tried to talk to her like we said. About the wedding, and she started talking about a Hunt and the darkness. Then her eyes, I don't even know, it was all so fast."

"It's okay, Emilia. We heard the screams and feared the worst. I'm glad you're okay, but I need to check on my mother. Lex, would you mind escorting Emilia back to my library, and stay with her till I'm done. I just want her safe."

"Of course, Cade." Lex nods and motions for me to the door.

"This isn't necessary," I tell Cade, who frowns at me.

"Please, Emilia. I don't want to worry about you too."

"Fine," I cave, I won't argue because of his mother, but I don't have to be happy about it.

I leave the room with Lex on my heels, but he quickly matches my pace stride for stride, and so I slow. There's no point trying to outrun him. Cade wasn't lying when he called him bearish, he's more the size of a bear than human. I've not really paid much attention to him before now, but his arms are painted in tattoos, and one in particular draws my attention. An eye inside a dreamcatcher. It's so irregular, but I feel like I've seen it before. I trip over my own feet because I focus on it so closely, and Lex catches me.

"Thank you," I murmur.

"Maybe you should pay attention to what's in front of you."

"What is that?" I point to the dark ink on his arm.

"It is something from the old world, a family thing," he tells me, brushing me off and opening the door to the library. "I'll be just out here if you need anything."

"This really isn't necessary, you know."

"Isn't it?" He shuts the door and leaves me in the dull light from the fireplace. This room holds so much history, things I don't know, things I probably don't care to know, but I wonder if there's anything in these books that can help us now. Tell us how to move past all of this destruction and pain. How to help Lanora. How to stop what is inevitably going to be another war, after we just stopped the last one.

"This fucking sucks." Rohan storms into the room and throws himself into one of the chairs like a petulant teenager.

"You got banished too?" I take a seat opposite him, enjoying the heat from the fire.

"Like a bloody child. She's my mother too, and it's not like I'm not a grown-ass man, but to defy the king is to defy the kingdom." He rolls his eyes and sinks further into the chair.

"Maybe he just wanted to spare you the pain of seeing your mother like that?"

"Maybe, or maybe he's just on a power trip. He's going to be king now, and it's gone to his head."

"Oh, come on, Rohan." I scoot forward and really pay attention to him. "You don't really believe that, and we both know it. What else is going on with you?" I carefully watch as he shifts in his chair, I notice his tired eyes, the lines on his face, and the hollowness of his cheeks.

Something is eating at him, and I've been so wrapped up in myself, I haven't noticed.

"Nothing really, just making sure everything is sorted here, and in the cities. I've just been spreading myself thin, I guess."

"I'm sorry I've been a bad friend recently, I've been so wrapped up in myself and everything going on, I've not checked in with you."

"Don't sweat it, Em. You've had shit going on, plus Erion is here. You've been busy, I don't hold it against you."

"That's no excuse though, you were the only person on my side when I came here. You stood up for me, you made sure I was safe, and I basically abandoned you. So, I'm sorry. After all this madness at the weekend, we should have a day, just us, what do you say?"

"I'd really like that." He smiles a tired smile but takes my hand and squeezes. "I kind of missed you, I guess. It's been lonely around here with everything happening."

The door opens, and Cade and Lex enter solemnly. "What happened?"

"She wasn't breathing. Whatever is plaguing her is killing her slowly. We brought her back, but the healers put her in a deep sleep while they try to work out what is wrong with her." Cade stands behind me, and kisses the top of my head before leaning on the back of the chair, while Lex stands stoically by the door as if guarding the room. "They think she's been poisoned."

"What?!" Rohan shouts and starts pacing the room. "How is that even possible?"

"I have no idea." Cade drags his hand down his face before taking Rohan's seat. "That's just one of their theories. It means she's not going to be up and about this weekend though, so we might need to postpone everything."

I nod and curl up in the chair. What a mess.

"She wouldn't want that," Rohan pipes up. "If she was herself, she'd hate that you postponed what is for the good of the court for her, and you know it."

"It's bad enough that Father is gone, but doing it without Mother too just feels wrong." Cade sighs.

"You and Emilia are the most important people this weekend. Both courts are a buzz about it, just the thought of a celebration has lifted the people, across the entire kingdom. You can't take that away from them, not after everything," Rohan stresses.

"I think he might be right," I tell Cade. "Lanora would want what is best for the kingdom. She also hates being seen as weak, so she'd hate you thinking like this. She will pull through, and who knows, maybe she'll be okay for the day."

"You're right. You're both right." Cade sighs in resignation. I watch as Lex stays silent by the door, but watches the brothers closely like he's trying to figure something out. "The show must go on."

16

*G*iven the recent awful events, everyone has thrown themselves into this, giving them something to celebrate. The Isle sees this as a sign of good fortune and happiness. I try not to let my grief overwhelm me, and keeping busy is the best way I've found to keep it buried, this is my duty as a princess, and is what my people need. In the past two days I've seen more food and cake than I possibly ever wanted to see, tried on more dresses than I care to recollect, been through color schemes, napkin materials, picked out the right china, flowers, suit options. So right now, I've shut the doors of my closet, and I'm hiding in here, just for ten minutes to escape the madness. I've not had a minute of peace, to think, or get hung up on the fact that I'm going to be celebrating my wedding in the room where my husband to be killed my twin brother.

I gulp in air and try to calm the panic rising inside of me. To top it all off, all of the Royal families from the Royal Courts confirmed their attendance, which means not only the parents of the girls who died here when the Hunters attacked, but it means my parents.

"Emilia?" I scoot backwards into the shadows as Erion opens the doors to the closet with a small smile, shaking his head as he walks in and closes the door, joining me on the floor in the darkness.

"How did you know I'd be in here?" I ask him quietly as he pulls me under his arm and hugs me tightly.

"I'm your big brother. I remember when things got too overwhelming when you were little, you'd hide in your closet, and when too many people clued in on that, you hid in mine."

"There's just so much, and everyone wants an answer yesterday. Do you have any idea how much food and cake I've tasted, how many dresses I've tried on…? So many people! People who a few years ago would've either spat at my feet or just ignored me completely."

"Well, you don't have to do it all alone, ya know, kiddo. I'm here now, I can help."

"But I don't want to intrude, Erion. You've got enough on with little Erion, who I'm just going to call E or Junior soon because calling him little Erion for the rest of existence is going to get tedious."

"You, Emilia, are my little sister, and I'd do anything for you. I missed a lot with you too while I was away, and

I'm sorry for not being there for you, or being there for you to lean on, but I'm here now."

"I love you, Erion. I missed you so much." I wrap my arms around him in the small space.

"I love you too, Em. I missed you too."

"I have something to ask you…" I pull back and face him. "I know you've not been here, but you're probably still the person I trust the most with almost everything. We've missed a lot up until now, but I want you with me in the rest of my important memories. So, I wondered, I mean, you don't have to, but I'd love it if you'd walk me down the aisle on Saturday."

"Oh, Emilia, I'd be honored." His voice cracks as he hugs me again.

"Thank you." I squeeze him harder again and swallow the lump in my throat. I haven't really had much chance to focus on the fact that he's back because life has been crazy, but the joy in this moment floors me.

"Now, let's get you back out there to face down the crazies and get this show on the road. We only have two days to get this thing done flawlessly."

"No offence or anything, Erion, but what use is a solider at planning a wedding?"

"Oh, you have no idea!"

I look at my reflection in the mirror, and I don't really recognize the girl in the mirror. She looks worldly, confident, regal. Like she's got her shit together.

"This is the one," Erion announces from the side of the room.

"You think so?" I whisper, trying not to think about how much Lily would have loved all of this. She'd have handled all of this wedding, coronation stuff a thousand times better than I have, and she wouldn't have looked flustered once. She'd have cried with me over finding the right dress, and calmed me down when the panic overtook me. I wipe away the tear that escapes and tip my head back to stop the others.

"Are you okay, Em?" Erion steps forwards and takes my elbow, guiding me off of the raised platform back to the floor. We cleared out my old bedroom and have used it as headquarters for all things wedding related. The wedding is tomorrow, and surprisingly, Erion has been a huge help.

"I'm fine, I'm just thinking about all of the people who should've been here but aren't. You would've loved Lily, she was the perfect ying to my yang. My complete opposite, but my best friend who loved me unconditionally. She was fierce but sweet, and I miss her so goddamn much."

"I'm so sorry, Emilia. But she's never really gone, you know that deep down. When we die, we go back to the earth, so the flowers that bloom in spring, the butterflies that flit around, she's here in all of that. She lives on in your memories."

"I know, it's just unfair. God, I sound like such a brat." I wipe the tears from my eyes. "I have so much, and so much more than others, but here I am crying when I'm about to marry the man I love."

"You're allowed to mourn, and even to be selfish, Emilia. It's not the worst traits of our kind. Plus, look at how far our courts have come in such a short space of time since it was announced that you and Cade were going to be married. People have been helping out others with rebuilding homes, pooling resources, and coming together to rebuild our communities. Plus, you've single-handedly planned this wedding and coronation while Cade has been spending time with his mother and making sure that the world keeps turning. It's a lot."

"Thank you for being here, Erion."

"Anything for you, baby sister. Now, seriously, this is the dress, and then we only have one thing left to do."

I can't help but laugh at his enthusiasm to be done searching for the right dress. I climb back up on the podium and take in the white and gold, silk and lace dress. It's so very simple and hugs all of my curves before flaring at the knee. Simple white silk topped with a beautiful gold lace that shimmers in the light.

"I think you might be right." I nod to the dressmaker in the corner who rushes to my side, pulling and pushing at the material, placing pins throughout it before telling me I can take it off. Erion leaves us at that point and waits outside while I dress.

I hurry to throw on the gown I had on before, apparently, queens to be don't get to wear jeans, stupid rule if you ask me. I now have people telling me what to wear and when to wear it, how to wear my hair, makeup, people who will do it each day. It's exhausting, there's so much that comes with being the face of a Court, so much more than I ever expected. I hurry and open the door to find Erion facing off with Lex.

"Erm, what exactly is going on here?"

"Nothing." Lex turns and stalks away from Erion, who I can feel the heat coming off.

"Hey"—I touch his arm—"calm down big brother. What just happened?"

"I don't trust that guy. Something isn't right about him."

"Oh, you don't have to tell me, after he and I had a little run-in." I involuntarily touch my neck. "I can't stand the guy, but Cade trusts him, and that's enough for me for now. He usually keeps his distance though, I've not seen him in this wing of the palace before."

"He was scoping out exits, counting steps. I recognized the movements from sieges I've done. Is he military?"

"I honestly have no idea, I try my best to avoid him. Now what was that last thing we needed to do?"

"Well, I'm not sure you need me for this last one, all

of the wedding stuff is done, and you don't seem so stressed now, but last up, is your crown fitting." His eyes sparkle with amusement.

"You are *not* leaving me alone with that creep! He is so handsy!" I exclaim. The Royal jeweler, Antonio, saw us yesterday for the ring fitting, and for some jewels to be encrusted in my shoes, and he just gave me the heebie-jeebies.

"Come on then, let's get this done, and then we have dinner with our new family before you're whisked away from your husband to be until the wedding."

He gives me his elbow, and I link my arm with his as he escorts me back to the sparkliest room I've ever been in. The vault holds all of the jewels that belong to the Winter Court, and holy crap are there a lot of them! We enter the vault again, and Antonio is waiting for us, a table laid with black velvet, holding six, very beautiful, very different tiaras and crowns.

"Oh, these are just exquisite!" I exclaim, drawn to the gold leaf tiara with red jewels, but something about it doesn't feel quite right.

"Thank you, Princess." Antonio blushes as he hurries to lift the tiara I'm staring at, while Erion hangs back, trying not to laugh.

"The three tiaras are your choices for the wedding, and the three crowns are what you'll exchange the tiara for during the coronation. I wanted you to have plenty of choices, but I didn't have as much time as I would've liked to make them."

"These are all made by hand?" I ask, wonder replacing the creeper feeling from yesterday.

"Yes, ma'am. Each one usually takes several weeks, but I just haven't slept for a few days, and I managed to get them finished."

"They're beautiful, Antonio. You should be proud."

"Thank you, Princess. Would you like to try each of them on?" I look over the others, and I see one with gold vines, frosted with white stones, and I know that it's the one.

"Just that one." I point to it. He passes it to me, and I place it on my head, pulling through some curled strands to hold it in place before moving to the mirror.

"It's stunning." I see Rohan behind me in the mirror at his words.

"It truly is," I agree, staring at it in the mirror, before Erion catches my eye and motions he'll be back, and I nod to let him know I'm okay.

"How are you feeling about tomorrow?" Rohan asks, stepping back and examining the crowns laid out for me.

"I'm excited, it's not something I ever saw for myself. At least not in recent years, and now it's here, and it's all so soon, but even with all of the devastation that happened to get us here, I wouldn't change a thing."

"You know, this time tomorrow, you'll be my sister, and I couldn't be happier for you and Cade. You deserve each other. I remember when you came back from the human realm as a child, and as soon as Cade saw you, he claimed you. He didn't have to say anything, but you could see it in the way he looked at you, the way he looked out for you. He still looks at you like that. God knows he gave me a shiner or too for looking at you too long. It's nice to see it all finally come full circle."

"Thank you, Rohan." I'm not too sure what to say to all of that. "I hope you are happy too."

His smile twists and he lifts the middle crown, it's gold and black, glittered with red, white, and blue stones, and it's beautiful in a dark way. "This is the one for you." He takes the tiara from my head and replaces it with the crown in his hands.

"A dark beauty, for the dark beauty that stole my brother's heart." He places it on my head, and it pricks my skin, making me wince. He lifts it and places it back down, and this time it doesn't hurt, but when he removes his hands, the weight on my head is heavy. "How is that?"

Antonio hovers behind us, clutching my tiara, looking nervous, and I smile at him to reassure him.

"It's beautiful," I admit. It is dark, but I quite like how it looks atop my head. I almost feel like a queen as I look at my reflection.

"Is this a private party, or can anyone crash it?" Cade strides into the room, Lex and Erion not far behind him.

"Oh, hi you. I thought I was seeing you after this." I

smile at him in the mirror as he wraps his arms around my waist from behind.

"I couldn't wait any longer, I've barely seen you this week, and well, that's it really. I missed you. I like this one, by the way." He nods to the crown on my head.

"We'll take this one too then I guess, Antonio, please." I take it from my head, and Antonio scurries over and grabs it before disappearing into another room at the back of the vault.

"Well, wasn't he just a little bit nervous. Let's get out of here, we have things to celebrate, and I want you to myself for a little while," Cade murmurs in my ear, and the other three leave us alone in the room.

"Hey." I smile at him, twisting in his arms to face him, and he kisses me, desperately, like I'm his air, and he can't survive one moment longer without his lips on mine. He walks me backwards until my back is pushed against the wall and entwines his fingers with mine, raising my hands above my head as he devours me.

"I have been waiting so patiently to get you alone when we're both awake." He grasps my wrists in one hand as he kisses down my neck, while his other hand lifts the skirt of my dress, exploring the skin he finds under there. I swear he growls when I whimper as his fingers graze my panties.

"Tomorrow, Emilia, and you will be mine fully. I'm going to do this right with you, but I need to feel you." He kisses me again as his fingers lift the lace of my panties and open me up. I gasp as his fingers enter me slowly, like some sort of sweet torture. It has been so long since I was touched like this, and Cade is setting my body on fire, and he's barely touching me.

"Tomorrow, you'll cry out my name, you'll pant and beg me to take you, but today, today I just want to show you what's coming." He pushes in deeper, hitting *that* spot, while his palm rubs on me, pushing me closer to the edge.

"That's it, Emilia. Let go for me." I whimper and bite down on his shoulder as I come undone on his fingers, grateful he's holding me up. He withdraws his fingers and pulls my panties back into place then lets down my skirts, still holding my hands captive. "That was beautiful." His eyes burn, and I feel the length of him as he presses up against me. I didn't think I could want him any more than I already did, but I was wrong, and my groan tells him how much I want him.

"Until tomorrow, Princess." He winks at me and steps back, adjusting himself. "Now, we have somewhere to be. Shall we?"

I wake in my old room and stare at the ceiling. I'm getting married today. And today I become queen. What a fucking day. I don't know if the butterflies in my stomach are excited or terrified, and the same goes for me, but I do know I'm anxious to see Cade again. Last night wasn't enough, and dinner was full of other people's chatter about today. I take a deep breath and sit up. Today is going to be a day I'll never forget, and I try not to groan at the thought of the drama my parents will undoubtedly bring with them. Other than their RSVP, I haven't heard a word from them. I still don't know if they know that Erion is here. But now is not the time to worry about that.

There's a knock at the door before it swings open, and Cybil enters with a silver trolley full of pastry treats, fruits, and Berripagne.

"Wedding breakfast for our soon-to-be queen." She smiles. I jump from the bed and hug her. I've not seen her since I was injured, but I know that she was visiting with her family. She might have been harsh with me at one point, but when I truly needed her, she was there for me.

"You're back!"

"I wouldn't have missed this day for anything. I've watched Master Cade for many years, I saw as he closed himself off from the world, but I've also seen him come back to that boy we all used to know since you've been back in his life, Emilia. For that, I thank you, and I want to apologize for my behavior when you arrived here. It was unnecessary and cruel, and I am truly sorry."

"You have nothing to be sorry for, I get it. You were being protective of the boy you helped raise. I can't really hold that against you. I should thank you for looking out for him when not many others were." She smiles at me and ushers me to sit as she places the goodies on the table in front of me.

"The girls will be here shortly to help you with your hair and makeup, and dress. So, enjoy this quiet while you can." She winks at me before she wheels the trolley from the room and leaves me in the peaceful calm again. I open the curtains and let the light of dawn into the room, the pink sky a beautiful sight.

I sit back down and indulge in a few gulps of Berripagne to try and calm the butterflies inside me before picking at the pastries. Too nervous to eat, I decide to jump in the shower, so I'm ready when the girls get here to make me look beautiful for today. I stand under the hot running water and try to wash away the stress and nerves, scrubbing my skin and hair until I relax. I shut off the water and climb out of the shower, wrapping a towel around myself. I grab the counter to steady myself as my vision blurs. Maybe I should've eaten more. I bend over and wrap my hair in another towel before padding out back into the room, where I find Rohan sitting eating my pastries and sipping on a glass of Berripagne.

"No indulgence spared today, huh?" He smiles cheekily, taking another bite from the sugary treat. "I just wanted to come and wish you all the best today—not luck because you don't need it, but I really do hope today goes to plan. For us all. I'd hug you but—" He motions to the fact I'm standing here, dripping in towels.

"Yeah, thanks." I laugh. "Are you ready for today? To stand up there beside your brother?"

"I am, and better still, the healers think Mother will be able to attend today."

"Oh, Rohan, I'm so glad to hear it! You and Cade must be so relieved."

"We are, we got news just before I came here. I was also asked to bring you this." He plucks a square velvet box from his jacket and places in on the table. I walk over to him, open it, and gasp. Earrings lay in the black velvet. Long drops that look like vines and the stones like leaves, perfectly matching my tiara. "A gift from your husband to be."

"They're stunning." I sigh as laughter filters through the door seconds before it opens, and Isabella and Eleanor appear through it with bags and boxes in their arms, ready to start prepping me for this day.

"And that"—Rohan stands—"is my cue to make myself scarce. I'll see you soon." He bends and kisses my cheek before making his escape from the room, the girls following him with their eyes, sighing at his departure.

"Are you ready to make me wedding-beautiful, ladies?"

J take a deep breath and look in the mirror. This is the day I've been waiting for my entire life, but now it's here, I don't know if I want it. Heavy lies the crown. I always thought it was the weak that used it as an excuse for their failures, but now I know it to be true. My father raised me to be a king, a soldier, a man ready to do whatever is necessary for my people. What he couldn't foresee was that Emilia would be the woman sitting opposite me, the perfect counterbalance for the cruelty he instilled in me.

Everybody is looking at us to be strong, to lead, to get us through what is to come. To join forces with the Summer Court as my father arranged, but with half of the Summer Court scattered to escape the fight that is coming, the weight sits firmly on my shoulders to make things right for our people.

Today I take the crown, I take the throne and everything that comes with the responsibility they both carry. With Emilia at my side to anchor me, my fear lessens about what we are going to face.

"Studying your pretty face pretty intensely there, brother." Rohan enters the room and clasps my shoulder in his hand. He may be younger than me, but these days you can barely tell. He almost matches me in height and size, and the darkness I tried to keep from him lingers behind his eyes. "Did no one tell you today is meant to be a happy day? The happiest of your life." He winks.

"Just making sure my beautiful face is matched in equal beauty by these dress robes." I laugh with him. He's wearing the same thing I am, but his are white instead of blue.

"You ready to be tied to one woman for the rest of your life?"

"I've been tied to her my entire life already, and you know it. Emilia bewitched me long ago, though I have to say our journey has taken a much different path than the one I imagined originally."

"Oh, I know. You are one lucky man, and the important thing is that you got here in the end. I know these last few weeks have been hard, saying goodbye to Father, dealing with Mother spiraling out of control, just trying to keep going, trying not to disappoint anyone, at the same time as helping our people rebuild and mourn while keeping them safe. It's been a tall order, but you've shouldered it well, big brother. He'd be proud of you. He definitely would've gone about it differently, but you're not as cold as he was."

"There's still time."

"Don't sell yourself short. And if you happen to stray off course, I'll be here to kick your ass back on the path." He knocks my shoulder with his and graces me a small smile.

"You know we're not meant to talk like this, right? If anyone heard us, they'd accuse us of spending too much time with the women in our lives."

"Maybe they'd be right, but fuck them. If I want a sappy moment with you, then I'll damn well have one. You ready to go out and face your adoring public?"

I take a deep breath and nod, the gold buttons and accents of my suit and robe catch the sunlight as we move. "Let the games begin."

I push the door open and walk through the halls of the palace. My Palace. The weight of the responsibility that is about to officially be mine bears down on my chest, making breathing that little bit harder. Rohan stands beside me, shoulder to shoulder as we wait outside the lower doors to the ballroom. I can already hear the people as they filter in and take their seats, the society climbers wanting to see how they can get their hooks into us, the little family we have left at the very front, and then we've opened up the rest of the seats to anyone who wants to be here. The amount of security here is ridiculous, but it is necessary considering the threat that still exists beyond these walls.

I touch the sword at my waist, there more for decoration than use today, but I feel better with it at my side. I should be happy right now, excited, but I can't help the foreboding feeling in the pit of my stomach that tells me something isn't right. The doors in front of us open to the side of the altar in the ballroom, and a hush descends across the hall. We take our places, me front and center, with Rohan behind me and to the left.

"We are here today to witness the crowning of our new king, and to join him with his new wife." The Master of Ceremonies' voice rings out across the room, clear and crisp. "We have seen much sorrow in recent days, but this day is the start of a new journey, of a new path. One of happiness, prosperity, and love."

The string quartet starts to play, and I smile inwardly, of course, she picked this song. It was her favorite years ago, the one I taught her to slow dance to before the first ball she was allowed to attend, since neither of her brothers would. I wait as the music plays and the doors open, but the person I see there isn't the one I want to see.

Erion rushes down the aisle to me and pulls me aside.

"What's wrong?" I ask amid the noise of the chapel.

"It's Emilia. She's gone."

I'm not sure how I got to this point in my life, but I don't think I ever did anything to deserve this. The Wild Hunt isn't meant to haunt the Fae, it is meant to serve no one but the dead, and our magik is meant to protect us. I never even believed it to be real, just another childhood story to induce fear and ensure compliance. I wish I'd paid more attention to my grandmother's stories when I was a child. Maybe then I wouldn't be here, trapped in this room, my clothes nothing more than sodden rags, or at least I'd know how to get out of here, wherever here is.

I couldn't even tell you how long I've been here. The constant darkness makes it hard to keep track of time, they come every now and then and try to speak to my mind, to read my memories, though I have no idea why.

I hear the clinking of his metal keys and crunching of

his boots on the dirty floor. He's coming for me again. I try to make myself small, as I curl into a ball in the corner, the wall at my back. I hold my breath as the steps get closer. I try to stop the tremble in my hands, the evidence of his last visit still shows on my arms, the dried and crusted blood in patches on what was once my beautiful wedding dress. I try not to whimper at the thought of Cade standing there, waiting for me, and me never showing. I hope he doesn't think I just ran, I hope with all that I am that he knows how much I love him, how excited I was to be his wife.

The turn of the key in the lock makes me flinch, and I scold myself internally. I will not show weakness in front of these monsters. I breathe slowly, fixing the walls around my mind as Grandmother taught me all those years ago. I don't know what he wants, but I am not going down without a fight. He steps into the room, lit only from the lantern in his thick hand. The light bounces off of the stone walls and shows me his emotionless face.

"Hello, Princess." I hear his scratchy voice inside my mind, and clutch either side of my head to try and stop the pain that follows. I scream out at the needles inside my skin. It doesn't matter that I can't see them, I feel them. "Are you ready to show me what you know?"

"I don't know anything. I don't understand, the Wild Hunt does not torture. They once took people to join the Hunt, none of this makes sense," I plead, and hear his throaty laugh as it echoes around the empty room. He takes a step toward me, and I scramble back up against the wall, trying to keep the distance between us. I watch as he tilts his head, trying to work me out. He pauses and just watches me, and then I feel it, the assault on my mind begins, as does the feeling of flames licking at my hands as I take my head in them to remind myself it's not real. I feel rather than see his approach, my eyes burst open as he lifts me from the ground by my throat.

I scratch at the hand around my throat and try to suck in the air. His grasp is too tight, and despite my fight, he stands, fixed to the floor. His dark, soulless eyes stare into mine. I drown in the darkness and feel as he starts to absorb the light within me. I see flashes at the corner of my eyes, as reality starts to fail me, and I swear I see Cade. There's no way he could be here. He couldn't be the reason I'm here. Could he?

I think back over the last few weeks, and try to make sense of it all, but the pain inside my skull is too much, and the little air I had isn't enough anymore. The burn in my lungs screams, and I lose the little hold I had left. I feel his smile as the world fades away, Cade's face the last thing I see.

"What is wrong with her?" I hear the voices, but I can't clear the darkness.

"She is resisting, and we need her not to. We need him here. He is the key to unlocking it all."

"But isn't she the one?"

"Yes, but without him, it's hidden."

"He didn't want her to know. Any of them to know, until it's time."

"We may not have a choice."

The pain inside my head returns when I wake, and I'm back in my cell. The yellow eyes of my captor stare back at me, glowing in the darkness.

"Good, you're awake."

"Oh good, he speaks." I try to move my fingers to keep the blood flowing and stop the pins and needles.

"Do not sass me, girl." His growl is amplified by his quick movement towards me, and I feel his breath on my face.

"You think this is sass, oh my, what a sheltered life you've lived." I mean, I probably shouldn't provoke the Hunter who has me captive, but at this point, what do I have to lose? "And so, the Hunters joined the Hunt. How very cliché."

The pain inside my head amplifies, and I scream out. The metallic taste of blood hits my tongue as it runs from my nose. It stops, and in the shadows, I see him again. The one from before.

"Good to see you're brave enough to be here alone, Hunter." His hand stings my cheek and rattles my bones as it connects with my face.

"Do not speak out of turn, Princess. You have no power here. This place was created a millennia before your pathetic existence." I reach inside myself to my fire, and I feel it there, a low flame, but I can't draw on it. For fuck's sake, where the hell am I?

He laughs, and I notice the door is open. And the person that walks through it is the last person I expected, the betrayal burns.

"Oberon…" His name falls from my lips as a whisper, but he doesn't look how I remember. His hair is longer, wilder, and his once beautiful face marred by scars, which could only mean he was burned and left unable to heal by magik. I can't help the sorrow that burns through me for what he must have suffered at the hands of my father.

"Emilia, I'd say it was good to see you, but since I can only see half of what I could, I can't really mean it." He drags his hair back and shows the melted skin where his eye used to be.

"I am so sorry," I gasp. "I tried to save you, I swear I tried."

"By shacking up and whoring yourself to the boy king? Oh yeah, I'm sure you tried really hard." I feel as his rage burns through him, and my poor shattered heart breaks a little more. "Bring them in here."

I watch as my parents are dragged into the room,

beaten, half-alive, and just barely breathing. I can't move as they shackle them to the wall, hung by their wrists, toes just able to reach the floor. I am torn between my desperation to save them, and my hatred at them for creating this entire situation.

"Please, you don't have to do this. If you could just tell me what it is you want from me, I can help, I'm sure of it. Nobody else needs to die because of the bigoted hatred of a few. Please." I lock eyes with Oberon and plead silently, trying to reach the piece of him that loved me once, but all I see is rage. Nothing but anger and hatred. He nods to the beast in the shadows that tortured me, and I watch on helplessly as my parents scream and writhe in agony. I scream for them, scream till I'm hoarse, but my pleas fall on deaf ears.

"I never meant for any of this," I cry once the screams stop, the silence almost as painful as the noise. "I loved you, Oberon. I fought to save you. I know you loved me too. That you must still care for me deep down as I once cared for you."

"You mean nothing to me, Emilia, so stop with your pathetic groveling. I never loved you, I needed you, needed what's inside your head. What we had was never real. We were never going to run away and be happy, in the human realm or any realm. If I'd have gotten you away from that place, it would have only been to bring you here, to him. You stupid, little girl. You have lost, but you will still give us what we need."

The last threads of string holding my heart together snap, and the pain I feel is worse than I ever thought.

"And now, I will take your parents, the same way I took the light from your beloved Lily, until you give me what we need."

"I don't understand," I cry, my pain and anger tearing through me, cutting my soul to ribbons.

"Don't you see, Emilia? All of this wasn't about me at all. All those lives lost, all those families torn apart, all those loves lost. It's all because of you. You hold inside you the key to everything."

"I'm glad you didn't finish the party before I arrived, boys. What a shame that would be! I left as soon as I could and diverted what I could, but I wasn't followed. Have you got very far?"

No. I refuse to believe it. This has to be a trick.

"We were just getting started, but breaking her isn't going to be easy. We'll find the location of the origin, sir. It just might take a while, and she might not survive it. It depends on how much it takes to reach the repressed memories. If she fights, she could lose herself inside her mind. It depends on how deep we need to go."

"Well, by all means, don't let me stop you. I need to get back to my brother, keep up appearances and all that. See if he's announced his missing princess yet." He laughs before he looks at me.

"It's okay, Emilia. I'm sure you'll survive this.

Though, if I get what I need from you, it won't matter either way."

"I don't understand. Wh-what is going on?" I stutter. This can't be real.

"What's going on, my dearest princess, is the plan I put in place so long ago. Everybody underestimated me. My father. My brother. No one truly knew what I was capable of. Then I found out about my whore of a mother's affair with none less than a Hunter, creating me. An abomination. But you see, when you were whisked away to the human realm with your grandmother, it was to help you forget. Forget what you saw. Forget the secrets you were destined to hold. The secret that holds the key to the power over the races. The reason for the Elves to be the mortal enemy of the Fae for so long. It didn't take long to find Hunters to join my cause. The powerful so long repressed when we should be at the top of this food chain. The Fae have ruled in comfort for too long while my kind have suffered. Your father put a dent in my plans, but all it took was a whisper or two in my father's mind, and my new plan was hatched. I'd have you close, to win your trust. To control your movements, navigate the game so that you would win. All so I could get you here. Maybe some of it wasn't necessary, but watching you was too much fun. Watching you think you were falling in love. Watching you believe you had your friends back. That you'd finally found your corner of happiness. You almost made it too easy to rip it from you, but I needed to break you, so I could reach in your mind and take what I needed."

"But I trusted you…" It's all I have. I don't know how to get back from this. I watch as he turns his back on me and walks from the room.

"Rohan! Rohan, don't leave me here!"

ABOUT THE AUTHOR

Sloane Murphy is the author of the international bestselling series, The Immortal Chronicles, as well as a range of other paranormal and contemporary romance. Sloane lives in Peterborough, England, with her husband & fur baby and over the years, she has developed an unhealthy appreciation for cheesy YA Films, cupcakes and bad pop music. She adores fairy tales, ballet and all things supernatural, drinks far too much coffee, and watches an ungodly amount of Netflix. When she's not busy writing, she can be found exploring the world with her husband and chocolate Labrador.

If you would like to send Sloane an email, you can reach her at sloane@authorsloanemurphy.com

Want to sign up for her mailing list? You can sign up at www.authorsloanemurphy.com

Or come join her reader group on Facebook, Sloanes Little Monsters

facebook.com/sloanemurphybooks

twitter.com/SloaneMurphyBks

instagram.com/sloanemurphybooks

bookbub.com/authors/sloane-murphy

ACKNOWLEDGMENTS

This book has been a labor of love, sweat, tears and tantrums. Not going to lie, so many times did I nearly give up on this re-release.

I have to say a massive thank you to Andie M Long for the wizardry you did on this book, it never would have started re-writes without you!

To Jenna, who without our sprint sessions, I never would've completed the words I needed to, thank you for pushing me!

Finally, to my readers, this is for you. Thank you for sticking with me, for your patience and loyalty, and for all your love. Without you, this all means nothing!

Dark Fae

(Paranormal Romance. Dark Fantasy)

Summer Princess

Standalones

When We Fall (New Adult Contemporary Romance)

OTHER WORKS FROM HUDSON INDIE INK

Paranormal Romance/Urban Fantasy

Stephanie Hudson

Xen Randell

C. L. Monaghan

Sci-fi/Fantasy

Brandon Ellis

Devin Hanson

Crime/Action

Blake Hudson

Mike Gomes

Contemporary Romance

Gemma Weir

Elodie Colt

Ann B. Harrison

Lightning Source UK Ltd.
Milton Keynes UK
UKHW010632040522
402481UK00001B/166